To C...

TERRIFIC TROUSER TRUMPETS!

Gorgeous George

And the Timewarp Trouser Trumpets

By

Stuart Reid

Illustrations, Cover and Layouts
By John Pender

Gorgeous Garage Publishing Ltd
Falkirk, Scotland

Copyright ©2018 Stuart Reid

The rights of Stuart Reid to be identified as the author of this work and the full Gorgeous George series has been asserted by him

Cover design and illustrations by John Pender
Cover and illustrations copyright © Gorgeous Garage Publishing Ltd

Photographs used by kind permission of
Betty Logan and John Pender

First Edition
This edition published in the UK by
Gorgeous Garage Publishing Ltd
ISBN 978-1-910614-11-2

www.stuart-reid.com

CONTENTS

Prologue

1. History
2. Farmer's Market
3. Jock and the Bean Shock
4. George's Turn
5. Chemistry
6. Doing the Can Can't
7. Cracker!
8. Been
9. Mean
10. Green
11. Ship Ahoy!
12. Who?
13. Wonderland
14. Tea
15. Wee
16. Home Alone
17. Toes
18. Comic book
19. A Cheeky Cheesy Chapter

20. Physics
21. Colours
22. Home Alone 2
23. Geography
24. Rainbows
25. Aztecs
26. Blame game
27. Me too!
28. To beez or not to beez
29. Ancient Egypt
30. Something wicked this way comes
31. Cave
32. Ancient Aliens
33. Ancient Eejit
34. Bubble, Bubble
35. Toil and Trouble
36. Greed

Epilogue

Epilogue Extra

Prologue

Don't skip this bit!

It has come to my attention that some cheeky readers often skip the prologue; one teacher even told me that SHE skipped the prologue too! We authors put this bit in for a reason... so start reading ... here...

GO!

So, little reader, what sort of madness are you looking for in these pages? Pirates, pyramids and pants full of poo? Superheroes with soggy, smelly socks? Time travelling toilets?

Maybe you want a book so exciting it'll keep you up past your bedtime, scared to put it down in case the adventure goes on inside the pages, on its own, even after you've stopped reading. A book that forces you to read on under the covers with your torch, long after your mum has told you to switch out the light twice already and you are now 'on your final warning'?

Well, little reader, you may have just found that book. And I hope you don't mind me calling you 'little reader'. You are reading after all, and there's a good chance you are smaller than me. I haven't met any people your age as tall as I am... in fact I'm taller than 97% of the entire population of the world.

So there! Na na na-na na!

There are some people in the world taller than me but they're called oddities. These weird giants walk around with snow on the top of their heads, icicle boogers dangling from their nostrils and feet so big entire tribes of mice live in their old shoes at the back of the wardrobe, despite the smell. Or maybe because of the smell. Mice love cheese, after all.

So if you are reading this book in your bed and it's night outside, you might just want to imagine somewhere out there, in a dark and gloomy corner of the world, there just might be a small leprechaun with gold teeth, eating curry from a dirty black cauldron.

And if you creep out of your bedroom and sneak around to this quiet corner of the world, hidden in the midst of a black cave, where even the moonlight is too scared to enter, you might tip-toe closer and hear this little green man mutter the most disgusting language you can imagine, as he struggles to push a large cow's bottom into the cooking pot.

You might also see this small freaky man, dressed in green britches and slender white stockings, strip off his jacket, lay down his spoon and begin smearing butter around the cow's bottom. Then you may just catch a glimpse of this leprechaun heaving his shoulder against a pair of saggy cow buttocks and pushing as hard as his magical little arms would allow. With a satisfying PLOP! the cow would vanish into the cauldron and the leprechaun would dance off into the night.

And, little reader, you might think this was all slightly odd.

Chapter One - History

Present day

'It's up here somewhere!' bellowed a voice from the darkness. Thick clouds of dust billowed around the attic and pinpricks of light caught specks in their beam. Boxes were piled high and newspapers spilled onto the floor.

'Are you sure you know what you're looking for, Grandpa?' yelled George. The only reply was more banging, thumping and muffled swearing, followed by the slow squeak of a high-pitched pump. Better out than in, Grandpa Jock always said.

George rolled his eyes and looked down at the bundles of yellow, fading pages. He knew his Grandpa Jock was much too impatient to keep a proper scrapbook; that would involve delicate cutting and snipping of articles, pasting, dating and cataloguing them correctly. Instead Grandpa Jock just kept all his newspapers, whole, intact, in a box in a pile in his loft.

The headline on the first Little Pumpington Chronicle read…

'Camouflaged Army Truck Disappears!'
George giggled to himself *'that's the whole point'* he thought, and picked up the newspaper to read the rest of the article. It was dated '26th August 1941' and explained how an experimental military vehicle vanished, apparently into thin air, after being painted with special green and black camouflage colours. In the corner was a small black and white photograph of a young sergeant with a large, bushy moustache and a mischievous glint in his eye.

'Grandpa?' shouted George, 'Were you in the army in 1941?'

Grandpa Jock's head popped up from behind a pile of boxes at the back of the attic. '1941? Do you think I am some sort of time traveller?' and he winked at George with a mischievous grin, before disappearing behind the boxes again.

'But the guy in this photo looks like you, Grandpa.'

More thumps, bangs and the clattering of piano keys.

'S#%$$^@&$,' came back the unusually high-pitched reply. 'Aargh, my thumb!'

George decided to leave it there. There'd be plenty of time for questions later. His Grandpa Jock had been up in the attic for almost an hour, searching for whatever it was he was looking for. Once he had an idea in his head there was no stopping him and George had learned it was usually best to stand well clear and wait for the dust to settle.

Gorgeous (or rather, not-quite-so-gorgeous) George Hansen was a pupil at the built, then destroyed, then rebuilt, then torched Little Pumpington Primary School; not totally scorched, just a little singed around the edges. And it wasn't George's fault. He'd actually tried to put out the flames using the vast sea of snot that just happened to be oozing around the school at the time. But that's a whole other story.

That week George had been staying over at his grandpa's house, recovering from a rather nasty bout of measles. George's mum and dad both worked long hours, and it was agreed that Grandpa Jock should look after his grandson for a few days whilst the spots cleared up.

George had spent the last few days sniffing and sneezing, and scratching at the bright red rash that covered his whole body. He even had little white spots inside his mouth, and he had hardly eaten anything for days.

On that particular morning, George had been launching himself from a battle bus and killing zombies on a video game that was too old for him (but Grandpa Jock didn't mind) when his grandpa, who'd been sitting quietly licking the coffee froth from his enormous ginger moustache, leapt in the air and yelled 'Holy flying cows, George, it's today!'

He spilt the rest of his cappuccino down the front of his kilt as he jumped from his chair and bolted up the stairs; his hairy little legs taking the steps two at a time. He pulled the ladder down from the loft and without stopping to look he leapt over the first pile of boxes and started rummaging.

George had waited patiently for ten minutes (well, he was going for a high score) until curiosity got the better of him. The banging and clattering was getting worse, and it seemed like the mad old Scotsman upstairs was nowhere nearer to finding his prize.

George had climbed up the step-ladder and hauled himself into the darkness. Grandpa Jock's attic was a treasure trove of mysterious artefacts, sealed boxes and wooden chests secured with chunky padlocks. Mountains of newspapers were bundled up in stacks all around and a large moose head was propped on top of one particularly precarious pile.

George now flicked through the other newspapers in the first stack. There were copies of the Roswell Daily Record in 1947, the Loch Ness Advertiser from 1933, and an English translation of the Tunguska Times from 1908, as well as an edition of a Spanish newspaper that George couldn't understand. On the front page there was a picture of his grandfather, beaming madly and gripping a viciously ugly creature that could only be described as a cross between a lizard, a monkey and a rabid chicken. The headline read *'Muchas Gracias, El Chupacabra Jocko'*. George made a mental note to Google these headlines and titles when he went back downstairs.

'YA BEAUTY!'

George dropped the newspaper and turned towards the darkest corner of the attic. A large chest was propelling itself up and over the boxes, followed closely by the flaming thatch of a grinning grandparent. Grandpa Jock emerged, biting onto one of those little reading torches and the light bounced around his face as he fought to hold it in his mouth. Occasionally his false teeth rattled but he couldn't stop smiling.

'What have you been looking for, Grandpa?' chuckled George, returning his smile.

'I just remembered, laddo, the Little Pumpington Players are rehearsing for their Christmas pantomime today,' shouted Grandpa Jock, hauling open the lid of the chest.

'So?' questioned George.

'So! I promised I'd look out this costume for them.' And Grandpa Jock held up the most moth-eaten outfit George had ever seen. It was a black and white splattered pattern and the trousers seemed to have hooves attached. Only when Grandpa Jock brought out the comically large head, complete with the rolling eyes and a pink, floppy tongue did George realise what it was.

'A cow costume?' gasped George. 'What are you doing with a pantomime cow costume in your attic?'

'I haven't used this for years,' gaped Grandpa Jock. 'Saved my life once or twice too.'

George shook his head in disbelief. How could a cow costume save someone's life? Grandpa Jock never ceased to amaze his grandson and he seemed to be able to find anything in his attic. George thought he understood his grandpa but a whole undiscovered history lay hidden in these boxes and George wished he knew more about him.

'Er, Grandpa?' George pointed down to the large damp patch on the front of Grandpa Jock's kilt.

'Have you wet yourself again, Grandpa?'

'Don't be daft, laddie,' chuckled Grandpa Jock. 'It's just coffee.'

'And what are you going to do with the costume now,' asked George, a little nervously, unsure if he was going to be part of a cow's bottom before the day was out.

'I'm not going to do anything with it,' announced Grandpa Jock proudly. 'You're going to take it to the theatre and give it to those actor chaps. The fresh air will do you good, boy.'

'What are you going to do when I'm away?' asked George, always suspicious about the mad ideas that might enter Grandpa Jock's head when he was left on his own for too long.

'I'm going to make us some dinner. All that searching has made me rather peckish. And you must be hungry too. Has your appetite come back yet, lad?'

'Certainly has, Grandpa, but what are you making?' groaned George, all too aware of Grandpa Jock's love of spicy food and the inevitable after-effects.

'Never you mind, boy,' replied Grandpa Jock, bending down to drag the chest to the hatchway. Parp! 'Help me get this down and you can head into town with it.'

Chapter Two - Farmer's Market

Present day

George carefully tied the ancient old box on the footplate of his scooter with old rope and slowly hauled the cow costume up the hill towards the theatre. It was some distance away and heavy going; at least once the box was dropped off but George thought at least he'd be able to scooter downhill on the way home.

Unfortunately, things never quite work out as planned for George. When he arrived at the theatre he was met by two strange thespian characters who liked to call themselves Bohemian Brian and Alan the Actor. They were a flamboyant pair, who wore the brightest, flouncy shirts and incredibly tight trousers. Brian was almost seven foot tall, whereas Alan struggled to reach Brian's belly button in his platform shoes.

They explained that although they were grateful for Grandpa Jock's kind offer of the cow costume, they'd had a slight change of plan, and rather than their Christmas play featuring a cow, they wanted to have a pantomime horse instead. They'd rewritten the script to include old jokes about horse burgers, horsey-kebabs and spaghetti bolo-neighs. Apparently, there was one particularly 'hilarious' scene that featured a nervous pantomime horse tiptoeing through a Tesco's frozen food aisle, where even the fish pie contained 60% seahorse. During the re-enactment, Alan and Brian skipped around doing their best horse impressions.

George nodded politely, and smiled encouragingly at the parts where he thought he was supposed to laugh but in the end, George was still left with a big box of cow costume on his scooter. It was way too unstable to ride on and George was not looking forward to the long trek home.

A couple of times on the way home George almost lost control of the heavy load, fighting furiously to hold onto the handles and still keep the big wooden chest balanced. For a handful of beans George would've been grateful to give away his moth-eaten bovine burden but let's be honest, there's not much call for cow costumes in most little towns these days.

But just as he reached the edge of the waste ground (that was always covered in dog-poo) and opposite the row of garages offering 'automotive repairs' and 'tyre replacement services', George caught a flash of light from the corner of his eye. He turned, and his eyes narrowed, focussing in on a strange little stall beneath a massive banner. George was certain it wasn't there before.

George stared closely. It wasn't a stall after all, it was a wheelbarrow lying on its side and behind it stood a tiny little man, wearing a green hat. George wasn't sure if it was trick of the light or if the man actually had a tinge of green about his skin. He was beckoning George over with a wave of his hand, pointing at something on his wheelbarrow counter.

George looked around; his mum and dad had always made the whole *don't-go-with-strangers* message pretty clear to him but there were mechanics working in the garages and two football teams playing in the park. It was broad daylight, it was a very public place and the little man was no more than three foot tall. *What harm could it do?* The little man smiled at George and shook a small leather purse in the air.

George took care to wheel his scooter through the maze

of dog mess and soon arrived in the middle of the waste ground, beneath the enormous banner. The banner, which stretched easily 20 feet across and hung over 10 feet off the ground, read 'Farmer's Market' in big letters. Apart from the wheelbarrow stand, the little man and his leather bag, there was just one neatly stacked pile of car tyres behind him.

'Hi beez Tom,' giggled the little man, covering his mouth with his hand. 'Tiny Tom, if you will.' He was breathing heavily, with a slight rasp at the back of his throat.

'Hello Tom,' nodded George. 'I beez George. I mean, I am George.'

'This beez my farmers' market,' waved Tom, proudly showing off the big banner way above his head.

'It's not a very big farmers' market,' said George, looking down at the little man.

'I iz not a very big farmer,' replied Tom, smiling. 'And it beez not the size of the market that's important, so long as you finds what you're looking for.'

'I don't think I'm looking for anything right now, thank you,' shrugged George, adjusting the balance of his scooter.

'You beez wanting rid of that box, sir?' The little man's eyes sparkled green, and as he smiled George saw his teeth were made of pure gold. 'I beez the seventh son of seven siblings and I can make all your dreams come true.'

'Sounds a bit dodgy, to be honest,' said George, trying to look as casual as possible.

'In this bag,' Tiny Tom held up the leather purse, 'are all the Has-beans, Will-beans, Chilli-beans and Never-would-beans the world has ever seen. This could be your fortune, sir.' He shook the bag with an encouraging rattle and winked at George, his teeth glittering in the sunlight.

George stared at the purse. His scooter was heavy, the box was bulky and he still had so far to walk. It was only an

old moth-eaten cow costume and the little green man was promising riches.

But it was his Grandpa Jock's moth-eaten cow costume. It wasn't George's to give away. He paused for a moment, deep in thought. What would Grandpa Jock do?

George nodded.

Then George grinned.

'YES!' He thought, punching the air. Grandpa Jock would ditch this box of flea-bitten old rubbish faster than a one-legged man in a butt-kicking contest!

George thrust his scooter towards the little man. 'Here, untie this!' he yelled and began pulling at the ropes holding the box in place. Like most things in life, Grandpa Jock would usually dive in feet first, kicking and screaming, yelling Geronimo! at the top of his voice.

If there was adventure to be had, then Grandpa Jock was usually at the front of the queue. George was never quite sure how old his grandfather was; somewhere between seventy-four and ninety-six years old was the best guess, but he knew Grandpa Jock would want to pack as much fun, excitement, colour, risk and dare into the rest of his days and he'd hate to pass up an opportunity for a little bit of madness.

George paused for a second, and then blinked. He looked down at the ropes again, which were now hanging coiled on the scooter's handle bars. The box and the cow costume were stored carefully on top of the now-righted wheelbarrow, with the spare tyres piled on top.

'What.... How... When... ?' spluttered George in amazement.

'Hi beez a quick fitter,' grinned the little man, flashing his golden teeth at George. George looked down at the leather bag now pressed into his hand. 'And a deal's a deal, sir,' smiled Tom. 'Just be careful what you wish for.'

'Wait,' cried George, still grateful to be rid of his heavy cow costume and box. 'Just tell me, what're the spare wheels for?'

Tiny Tom laughed heartily, his mouth shining brightly as he illuminated the world.

'That beez my re-tyre-ment fund!' and in a flash, the barrow and the wheels, the cow costume and the box, the big banner and the little man were gone.

Chapter Three -Jock and the Bean Shock

Present day

The closer George got to his grandpa's house, the more doubts entered his head. Had he done the right thing? Had he given away a family heirloom? Sure, the cow costume had been up in the attic in for years but he didn't know how attached his Grandpa Jock was to it? Maybe it was worth something? Really valuable or just sentimental? Maybe his Grandpa Jock would go sort of mental because all he'd really gotten in return was a bag of old beans.

Would Grandpa Jock go mad? George thought his Grandpa Jock was already a bit mad but what if he was angry this time?

George gulped as he stepped through the back door. Rich, pungent smells smacked into his nostrils and he knew immediately that Grandpa Jock was conjuring up one of his killer curries; the kind that reminded you how spicy it had been the following morning. The kind of curries that gave your bum a bite on the way out.

'Erm, I'm s-sorry Grandpa,' stammered George, keeping his head down. 'I gave away your cow costume but er... not to the actors... to a little green man in the park.' George was suddenly aware how ridiculous it all sounded now. 'I got these beans for it though.'

Grandpa Jock was standing by the stove, stirring a large, bubbling pot on the hob; George stepped back. His grandpa's face was turning bright red and his teeth were clenched together; his jaw was set firm and his eyes were popping out of his head.

'Aaaaaargh!' growled Grandpa Jock. George had never seen him this mad before; there was practically steam coming out of his ears.

'Man, that's spicy!' wheezed the old Scotsman, gasping for breath and reaching for a glass of milk. He gulped down a mouthful and swirled the rest around with his tongue.

'Ah, that's better,' he said, still feeling the prickle of spice on his lips. 'Now, what were you saying? You got rid of that flea-bitten cow suit? Thank goodness for that.'

'So, you're not mad?' breathed George with a sigh of relief.

'Mad? I've been meaning to dump that thing for years,' winked Grandpa Jock. 'Now, let's see these chilli-beans then.'

Grandpa Jock took the bag from George's still shaking hand and emptied it out on the counter. The beans were green and gold, and they glistened as much as Tiny Tom's teeth. Grandpa Jock picked out a few of the larger ones and threw them into the pot. Sparks flew and little pops of stardust burst out of the pan, as the fumes rose.

'Heh heh heh, another famous curry night for the Hansen lads, eh boyo.'

Two hours later, Grandpa Jock and George both sat in front of the television with their bellies bursting, amidst the remnants of their dirty dishes, leftover naan breads and little pieces of poppadom crushed into the carpet.

'Aye lad, I love a good curry, me,' groaned Grandpa Jock, adjusting the belt on his kilt.

'Yeah, Grandpa, it was brilliant,' moaned George, glad that his black tracksuit bottoms had an elastic waistband. 'I reckon that was one of your best, Grandpa.'

Just then, Grandpa Jock sat up and put his hand over his tummy. He looked surprised.

'Ooh, did you hear that?' he said, turning to George. 'That gurgle?'

'No, I didn't hear.......' But George's words were drowned out by a loud, burbling slosh coming from Grandpa Jock's belly. Grandpa Jock jolted backwards.

'Urgh, that's got a bit of kick to it,' grunted Grandpa Jock. 'And sooner than I expected.' The gurgling rumbled again,

15

this time with a great deal more urgency. George laughed…

'You better be quick, Grandpa. We don't want any more 'accidents'.'

The old Scotsman staggered to his feet but no sooner was he standing than his tummy gurgled again, and he was forced to grip his bottom with both hands. His moustache began to shudder and there was a look of panic on his face. George began to stand up but it was too late…

A thunderous roar exploded from Grandpa Jock's butt and his whole body shook as the fearful flatulence ripped through him. Wave after wave of the biggest bottom burp that could ever befall a human being thrust its way out of Grandpa Jock's rear end until the kilt-clad old geezer finally shuddered to a halt. The air around him began to cloud over with a misty green haze and George covered his mouth and nose with his hands, as his Grandpa Jock was wrapped in a blanket of rancid cabbages.

Then Grandpa Jock disappeared!

George stared in amazement. His grandfather, standing in front of him just a moment ago, had completely vanished into thin air. Well, not exactly thin air… more like the *thick, choking, foul-smelling fumes from a sulphur factory* type of air… but none the less, he was gone.

Had he spontaneously combusted? Exploded into nothingness in the fumes of his own farts? Not possible, thought George, nobody blows themselves up with their own bottom burps, no matter how powerful their curry was.

George took a step forward and the stench hit the back of his nose; he gagged and almost saw his curry and naan breads again. He stretched out his hand (and held his breath) as he waved his fingers through the swirling green mist. His grandfather was definitely not in there. George couldn't stand the stink any longer and he stepped back.

There was a shower of green sparks and more sizzling

smoke, and Grandpa Jock was back in his living room, looking pale and shaken, and there were wisps of smoke curling up from the strands of hair around the top of his head.

He turned and looked at George, and he smiled. Then he began to chortle. He threw his head back and let out an enormous belly laugh that shook the room.

'Grandpa, where did you go?' yelled George, still not quite sure what he was seeing.

'It was me, George,' laughed Grandpa Jock. 'It was me. I started it!'

'Started what, Grandpa?' urged George.

'London burnt down in 1666, lad! It was me, I fanned the flames out of my butt.'

George stood and stared, his mouth agape. Had his Grandpa Jock really gone totally mad this time? He didn't really go back in time to the seventeenth century, did he? But he had disappeared for a few seconds there, so where did he go?

'When I dropped that whopper, George,' explained Grandpa Jock, 'for a moment I was surrounded by my own gaseous parp. I could see you and the room and the clouds. Then it went hazy, green sparks were flying and I suddenly found myself in an old-fashioned kitchen. I was there, I was actually there. The oven was enormous, I was back in time and there was flour everywhere.'

'Of course, I was too scared to move,' he went on, 'but I could just make out a sign above the kilns; it read *Thomas Farriner – Bakers, Pudding Lane, London.* But again, I couldn't hold my wind in. My bottom blasted, throwing sparks from the dying fire and the flour dust burst into flames.'

'As the green gas cloud wrapped around me again I could just make out the flames spreading wildly across the kitchen and it was then that I knew… I caused it, lad. I started the Great Fire of London.'

'But Grandpa,' George was still coming to terms with the whole disappearing/reappearing thing. 'You can't change history.'

'No but maybe I *caused* history, lad,' laughed Grandpa Jock wildly. 'And why would we go back and change it now. That's what happened, wasn't it? It's in the history books already. It's in the past!'

'Grandpa, the beans!' yelled George, beginning to realise the truth. *Be careful what you wish for*, the little Farmers' Market man had said.

'Yes, the beans,' nodded Grandpa Jock. 'Powerful enough to produce….' They stopped and stared at each other, before whispering together…

'…Time-warp trouser trumpets!'

Chapter Four - George's Turn

Present day

Time travel can be exhausting. Grandpa Jock had certainly turned a pale shade of yellow when he emerged from his gas cloud, and he was clenching something so tightly in his hand that his knuckles had turned white. He was in such a daze that the old Scotsman excused himself and headed up to his bed for a 'bit of a lie down'.

George stepped into the kitchen, mainly to escape the smell that still lingered in the living room. He was feeling slightly sick too but that was due to the smell, rather than the effects of an inter-dimensional time shift. He hadn't gone anywhere, only Grandpa Jock had jumped through the time-warp.

Why not? George argued with himself.

He had eaten just as much curry as his grandpa, maybe more even, so if anyone deserved to be blasted back in time by a great big bottom burp, it was him, surely.

He was still feeling rather full after his dinner. His fat little tummy was still pressing against his waistband and he certainly could not eat another bite. But then again, maybe that was the problem, he thought. Bottom burps are built up by gas in the intestines, as food breaks down inside the body, and beans, onions and spicy food can release large amounts of methane and hydrogen sulphide.

And then George realised. The reason he hadn't time-warped was he was still too full! There was no space in his tummy for the gas to escape. He took a jump to his left.

Then a step to his right. With his hands on his tummy, he squeezed his buttocks tight. His stomach gurgled.

But it was his tummy churning that really drove him insane. He crouched into a ball, hoping to relieve the stabbing pain in his belly. And as he crouched, *listen closely*, a small pump squeaked. The air shimmered around George, as a wisp of flatulence slipped out.

'It's astounding,' he thought. 'Time is fleeting. Madness is taking its toll.' Can people really travel through time? It was beyond belief.

'Not for very much longer,' George clenched. 'I've got to keep control.' He did not want to follow through!

And he jumped to the left. Then again, he stepped to the right. With his hands on his tummy, he squeezed his knees in tight. He shook his hips from side to side to free up the build-up of gas in his gut.

And this time, his stomach jumped. Not a big jump, but a little pop in the pit of his tummy. Then a jolt. A bigger jolt followed by an enormous gurgle. A big ball of spicy wind was making its way through his digestive system at, what George could only describe as, light speed.

'Let's do the time-warp,' George shouted, as a thunderous parp finally left his bottom, bursting through with the hyper-space capabilities of the Millennium Falcon.

And the Blackness did hit him… the void started calling… into another dimension, with adventurous intention, he squatted. A misty green haze wrapped around the small boy, almost crushing him with a depth of warmth and smell and texture, and he was into the time slip.

Sparks flew and space raced by. Strange lights and sounds and smells (mainly cabbage) blitzed his brain, as the colour of magic crackled green and gold all around. After seeing all this, George thought, nothing could ever be the same again.

Time was no longer a single line straight directly ahead but a spiral of loops and swoops; of mind-slips and time-slips. And eventually, the swirling mist began to clear; an old-fashioned kitchen slowly appeared.

A small brass sign above the huge black ovens read *Thomas Farriner –Bakers, Pudding Lane, London.*

'This is the baker's where Grandpa came out,' whispered George, to no-one in particular. 'But only… it's not on fire. Maybe I have time to save London!'

George looked around. Clearly he had arrived before the fire started and perhaps he had the chance to put right what Grandpa Jock's bottom had pooped wrong.

Beside the ovens were large wooden trays, laid out on the tables and filled with balls of dough, ready for firing in the morning. Each tray was covered in a thin layer of flour to stop the dough balls from sticking to each other. Embers in the grate of the fireplace still glowed orange and gave an eerie glint to the room.

But it wasn't the embers that caught George's eye. In the corner of the kitchen, behind the enormous sacks of flour piled up against the wall next to the oven, a faint green light sparkled. If it had been a few hours later, and daylight was shining into the bakery, then this glow would've been invisible, hidden by the sunshine. But here, in this dark and gloomy corner of the world, the green glow was allowed to stretch itself into the darkness.

George stepped across the flour sacks and reached behind the stack. Inside the small cloth bag were a few gold coins. Each one shimmered as if life itself was glowing within them.

He picked up a coin from the top of the pile. It was warm to touch, not hot but just enough to be pleasant on the skin. The coin glimmered in the faint light from the fire.

As he looked closer, George's eyes widened. He held the coin up to his face. He turned it over, then flipped it back again.

His face was one side!

George flipped the coin over again. On the tails side was an engraving of a strange animal, or at the very least, a strange animal's bottom pointing upwards. The head of the beast could be seen poking around the side, smiling.

He spun the coin back around. The face hadn't changed. It was still depicting a small boy with curly hair, one eye slightly bigger than the other. His nose was curled up and there were slight indentations on his cheeks, as if to signify freckles.

The coin itself was remarkable, with fantastic detail on both sides and in nearly mint condition… nobody had carried this around in their pocket. George felt the weight in his hand and reckoned it was about the same as a large slice of bread. The precious metal felt very heavy for its size.

He looked again at its face, his face, and gulped. What was this time-warp treasure trove? George bent over and lifted the sack of coins.

His tummy gurgled again. He clenched his buttocks.

It was too late.

Caught by surprise, George couldn't hold his wind in. His bottom blasted, and sparks from the dying fire were fanned across the kitchen. As soon as the sparks lightly touched the flour dust burst into flames, and began spreading wildly around the kitchen. The dry wooden trays went up like tinder. Fiery tongues licked around the walls and the beams running across the ceiling.

Time began to flicker again. Madness scratched at the sides of George's mind and the darkness warped around him, dragging him into the void. A burning stench followed him through the mists of time, seeming to cling to his hair and clothes, and George shut his eyes tight.

Suddenly, he was back in his Grandpa Jock's kitchen again. A large pan of cold curry sat on the hob and he stood there holding a bag of gold coins.

Then George realised; Grandpa Jock didn't start the Great Fire of London.

He did! George! With a big blast of sparks that practically flew of his arse!

And at this point, I should say sorry to all the mums, dads, teachers, librarians and anyone else who may be reading this book to a small child. That is the only use of the word 'arse' in this book, I promise. Just bleep over, if you don't like it… or use bum, butt, or bottom instead. Buttocks, backside, behind or bon-bons would also work. Gluteus Maximus is the correct phrase but Junk in Your Trunk is funnier, and much less formal. My favourite is Badonkadonk.

Let's be honest… most kids use words 10 times worse that 'arse' in the playground anyway, you great big hairy badonkadonk!

And historically, the term 'arse' is Anglo-Saxon in origin, and over a thousand years old. It describes the two rounded portions of the anatomy, located on the posterior of the pelvic region between the lower back and the perineum of both apes and humans. There are several connotations of buttocks in art, fashion, culture and humour, and the English language is replete with many popular synonyms, though it may also used as an insult for a person. Shakespeare even had an ass called Bottom. See, this is educational.

Kids, be careful where and when you use this information. Badonkadonk is funny but arse will get you into soooooo much trouble!!

Chapter Five - Chemistry

Sunday 2nd September 1666

Gold can be such a distraction.

Gold can warp people's minds. Men have killed for it. Women have fallen in love with it. And throughout history, humans have searched for, and fought over, and died for, tiny little lumps of yellow metal.

It is not the rarest ore. Chemically, it is rather boring. But it does not rust in water, like iron, or tarnish in the air, like silver; and copper corrodes. But gold is unbelievably beautiful. It is soft, yet strong and shines like sunlight. The Incas believed gold to be "the sweat of the sun".

And gold absorbs. Gold steals the very essence of everyone it touches, and swallows it and holds it deep in its golden heart forever. Dark magic does not always need to be dark. Hiding in plain sight can fool those gullible enough to fall in love with the shiny, shiny, shiny.

Hiding in the corner of the bakery that night, in that year, was a very small man with a golden smile. A sly, impish snarl of a smile; he drummed his fingers together, and giggled…

"All that is gold does not glitter.
Not all who love it are lost.
But the ore that absorbs takes with it,
The heart, soul and spirit. The cost."

Chapter Six - Doing the Can Can't

Present day

Little Pumpington was a boring little town. Nothing ever happened there (apart from zombie epidemics, school explosions, poo-poisoned cheeseburgers and an out-of-control elephant sanctuary) and George had decided that nothing else exciting would happen there. The only excitement that George had in his lonely little world was listening to his parents arguing. And boy, could they argue?! Sometimes they could make one argument last for days... and days and days and days.

As soon as they were put in the same room together, it usually meant fireworks, lots and lots of fireworks, especially those loud, exploding ones that you can feel down in the pit of your stomach.

That was why George spent so much time visiting his Grandpa Jock. Grandpa Jock was completely and utterly bonkers, and if anybody was going to liven up life, then it was his mad Scottish grandfather.

Now, George was an odd-looking little chap, with red, curly hair and eyebrows way too bushy for a 10 year old boy. One ear was slightly bigger than the other, and one eye was slightly lower than its buddy. George was short and thin, but his podgy little tummy poked out at the front and his bum stuck out at the back. In fact, his bottom always looked too big for his body, as if it wasn't really his own.

But who has ever heard of a bum transplant!

Anyway, the next morning, George woke up later than usual. In fact, you could say he had slept in but since his Grandpa Jock hadn't shouted him down for a massive plate of bacon and eggs, then there was nothing to sleep in for.

Except...

The bag of gold coins sat on his bedside table. George sat bolt upright and turned to his left. It was really there. George stared at it, certain now that his time-jump was no longer just a dream. He had brought the proof back with him.

The coins shimmered in the early morning light, as if sunshine itself wanted to party as soon as it kissed the gold. And the coins weren't just *gold*, they were *Golden!* Gloriously golden, glinting and glimmering, and without doubt the shiniest coins George had ever seen.

Quietly, he tipped them out onto his bed and picked up each one in turn. They all had his head embossed on one side. He was sure it was meant to be him but he couldn't understand why. There were no other markings or words that might suggest a clue.

George knew that Grandpa Jock would certainly be able to help. Maybe he could take them to the museum… or maybe the answer was just a mystery lost in history.

'Hey, I'm a little poet,' thought George 'and I didn't even know it.'

'I can make a rhyme, any old time,' he went on, smiling to himself.

'Each rhyme I invent comes from the heart. Get ready everybody, for a time-travelling f-f-f…'

George stopped. He paused and thought for a second. It was really just a matter of time before his bottom blasted again, especially the morning after one of his Grandpa Jock's famous killer curries. And this time, he wanted to be ready for it. He wanted to enjoy time-travel, and maybe he could find out more about these coins.

So just to make sure, George jumped out of bed, ran downstairs and into the kitchen to search for any leftovers. Grandpa Jock always made too much and George loved nothing better than cold curry the morning after. The pot sat

on the hob with a crusty skin forming on the surface
of the sauce.

He snatched up a spoon, quickly scooped a dollop out of
the pan and gulped down the first mouthful… it was cold,
creamy, prickly, spicy, satisfying, then spicier, pricklier,
burny, hot, burning, burning… hot, hot, hot!

Without any rice or naan bread to soften the taste, the
curry was even more potent than it was last night. George's
tongue began to tingle and he let it droop out of his mouth
to catch the cool air. He was panting like a dog, trying
desperately to cool his mouth, before he opened the fridge
and took a long gulp of milk straight from the carton.
He held the cold liquid in his mouth until the spice on his
tongue settled down. There were beads of sweat now
forming on his forehead.

He scooped a little more of the curry into his mouth and
took another swig of milk. There were still some magic
beans in his bag but he didn't want to waste them until he'd
figured out how they worked, and his mind was ticking over
as he trotted back into the living room.

Poppadoms and naan were still crunched into the carpet
from the night before but George didn't care. His tummy
was gurgling gently and he knew it wouldn't be long until he
had another epic explosion.

But just then, there was a knock at the back door and two
children entered. Nobody ever waited at Grandpa Jock's
back door, everyone was always welcome.

'Good morning, George,' shouted the young lady, brightly.

'Good morning, you great big bag of monkey poo!'
laughed Kenny, as he fist-bumped his friend.

'Good morning too, Kenny. Still smelling like baby barf,
I see.' George was waving his hand in front of his nose
and sniggering.

Allison rolled her eyes. 'Seriously, you two. Is it not about time you both grew up?'

Allison Lansbury was a tall girl with dark brown hair. She was sharp, and smart, and witty, and had absolutely no idea why she enjoyed the company of these two idiotic morons. George could be smart and sensitive at times but Crayon Kenny just brought out the worst in him. Crayon Kenny brought the worst out in himself. That boy was nuttier than squirrel poo!

To begin with, he was given the nickname 'Crayon' because of his love for sticking crayons, and a whole variety of other objects, up his nose. (don't try this at home, kids). He was unpredictably idiotic and stark raving bonkers. And he was often seen drifting off into a tiny little world of his own. Goodness knows what he thought about.

'That's it. It's about time!' cried George.

'Good,' replied Allison.

'But I don't want to grow up,' added Kenny.

'No, it's all about time,' blustered George. 'Let me show you.' And he sprinted upstairs, returning shortly with his bag of coins. Allison's eyes widened. Kenny blew out a long, low whistle.

'Where did you find these, mate?'

'Not where. When!' replied George. 'In the year 1666 to be exact!' and he proceeded to explain last evening's entertainment to his friends. Kenny and Allison's mouths gaped wider and wider with every new piece of mad adventure. Allison shook her head. Kenny finally laughed.

'You're making that up,' he giggled.

'It's true, I promise,' insisted George. 'They were magic beans and we went back in time.'

'Right, let me taste this curry then,' said Kenny, marching into the kitchen.

'You won't be able to eat it,' argued George. 'It's much too spicy for you.'

'Yes I will,' snorted Crayon. 'I can eat anything.'
'No you can't,' grunted George.

'Yes I can!'

'Can not!'

'Can so!'

'Can't!'

'Can!'

'Can't!'

'Can!'

'Can't!'

'Can!'

'Can't!'

'Can!'

'Can't!'

'Can! Can! Can!'

'Can't, can't, can't'

Well, little reader, I suspect you may be rather irritated with this childish conversation by now. I certainly was, and went off to make myself a cup of tea and let the boys get on with it for a while.

Allison was irritated too, and ignoring the boys, she drifted off towards the cooker. The curry pot was sitting on the hob, and the brown sludge at the bottom was looking a lot more like mud and a lot less appetising.

'Is this it?' she asked, pointing at the mucky, brown mess that was caked to the sides of pan. 'Is this the time-travelling slop then?'

The boys stopped bickering and turned towards Allison. She had picked up a spoon and was carefully stirring it around in the gloop. Occasionally, little sparks would fly out of the spicy gunk.

'NO!' cried George and Kenny at exactly the same time; Kenny, because he wanted to prove he could eat spicy food, and George, because he wasn't sure what effect the leftovers might have on an untested time-traveller's intestines.

But before Allison could lift the spoon to her mouth, George grunted in pain and doubled over. He shuddered and shook, gripping onto the table to stop himself from falling over.

Then, his bum let out an enormous clap of thunder. It was like an orchestra imitating thunder on their big bass drums, rolling and rumbling. George's trouser trumpets were playing their own symphony in his underwear. No, not trumpets but drums and now trombones, dozens of trombones! Paaaarp!

And great big tubas (Paaarp!)… an entire brass section (parp, parp, parp!) and again the rumbling big bass drum to finish off with. George sank to his knees, exhausted.

The smell filled everyone's nostrils and they all choked. Everyone likes the smell of their gas but even George thought this was a bit too much.

The light seemed to shimmer, sparks crackled in the air and a green fog wrapped around the three of them.

'Grab my hands!' shouted George, as he reached out for Allison and Kenny, pulling them in closer. The smell was even worse closer to George and they both coughed. The air itself even seemed thicker but this was a trip neither of them wanted to miss.

The world that they knew began to disappear…

Look at that, little reader, three little dots.

That's called an ellipsis. Say it out loud - EE-LIP-SIS.

It means a deliberate literary pause, to let the reader think about what might happen next… like a little mini-cliffhanger.
When I see three little dots like that, I think DUN, DUN, DUN! in a very dramatic way, inside my head. Okay, let's try that bit again.

The world that they knew began to disappear…

DUN, DUN, DUUUUUN!

Chapter 7 - Cracker!

Thursday 15th September 1729

When Grandpa Jock woke up, it was dark. Not night-time dark; it was definitely daytime because he could see peeps of sunlight shining through his ears. Then he remembered. His head had been shoved down the barrel of a large cannon, right up to his shoulders! No wonder it was dark.

And there was something pecking at his hands (but what else should he have expected, this hadn't been a normal day.) Grandpa Jock shook his arms wildly and the pecking stopped.

He reached back and pushed against the cold, metallic rim of the cannon and heaved hard. A small 'Pop!' echoed inside the barrel and the old Scotsman wobbled, then fell over onto his fat little bottom. He sat there blinking as his eyes adjusted to the sunshine.

Grandpa Jock was sitting on the deck of a pirate galleon. He knew it was a pirate ship, as he could see the skull and crossbones flag fluttering off the bow. That, and the most motley crew of salty sea-dogs that ever set sail were jumping madly around, down at the other end of the ship. They were shrieking and hollering and waving their shiny cutlasses in the air. Another ship had just come into view and, luckily for Grandpa Jock, this had distracted their attention.

'Yarrrrr!' shouted the pirates.

'Aaawwkk!' said something else altogether.

Above his head, sitting proudly on a wooden barrel, was a bright blue and very yellow parrot. The parrot nodded at old Jock, and for some reason, Grandpa Jock nodded back. Then he turned towards the pirates again, who were still shouting angrily.

'Aaaaawwwkkk!' squawked the parrot.

'Shhh! They'll hear,' hissed Grandpa Jock, hoping the bird would keep quiet. The pirates didn't notice but then again, a parrot squawking on board a pirate ship is probably a common occurrence.

The old geezer struggled to his feet before he remembered that his legs had been tied together below the knees. He toppled over again, and shuffled on his bottom behind the cannon, out of sight. He did think it slightly strange that he'd forgotten he'd been tied up but that bang on the head must've been harder than he thought.

Bang on the head? He felt the lump throbbing on his temple and it all started coming back to him.

'Aaaaawwwkkk!' squawked the parrot again.

'Shhhhhh!' whispered Grandpa Jock, waving his hands at the bird in a desperate bid to quieten it down. The bird hopped off the barrel, fluttered down onto the deck and pecked at the ropes holding his legs together.

Grandpa Jock looked at his hands. His wrists were red raw, with blood-crusted scratch marks on his arms.

'My hands were tied too,' he gasped, watching the parrot pick furiously at the hemp. 'Did you free my arms? Could I feel you pecking when my head was stuck down the cannon?'

'Aaawwkk!' croaked the parrot, slightly softer this time and Grandpa Jock was sure he saw the parrot wink.

The rope started to fray and Grandpa Jock pulled at the loose ends until he could wriggle his legs. Slowly the bindings fell away and he was free at last.

Grandpa Jock reached round into his sporran and felt for his mobile phone. It was still there but the battery was totally dead. As he stood up, the parrot jumped onto his head and hopped up and down furiously until Grandpa Jock crouched down behind the barrel, out of sight.

(Sorry to butt in here again little reader but 'a sporran' is the little hairy bag that Scotsmen wear with their kilts. There are no pockets in a kilt so a sporran is required to keep your keys, your wallet and your mobile phone handy.)

'Okay, okay, I get the point,' he mumbled, realising the bird wanted him to stay hidden. 'But I've just never been bossed around by a stupid parrot before.'

'Well, excuse me, sir. I wish to remove myself from this stinking ship as much as you do but getting yourself captured again will not help either of us, will it?' said the parrot. Grandpa Jock's bottom jaw hit the deck.

'You just spoke?' spluttered the old geezer, his bushy ginger moustache quivering on his top lip.

'Of course I just spoke. All parrots can speak!' replied the parrot.

'Yes but... but usually just, like, parrot-fashion.' Grandpa Jock stumbled over his words. 'I mean, just repeating phrases... *Polly wants a cracker*... and stuff like that.'

'As I said, all parrots can talk. We're just rather fussy who we talk to,' declared the bird, puffing out the feathers on its chest.

Chapter 8 - Been

Present day

Definitely not a normal day, thought Grandpa Jock... but maybe we should start at the beginning.

After his evening's entertainment, Grandpa Jock had stumbled off to bed, feeling rather tired. He obviously hadn't cleared all the gas from the last time, and no sooner was he lying in bed than his tummy began to gurgle again. Grandpa Jock steadied himself.

Now, most small boys, and many older men, seem to enjoy the smell of their own parps, especially in bed. Many of them often relish popping their heads underneath the duvet to inhale their fragrance. And then, nearly always, they will chuckle to themselves.

The only time that males stop doing this is when men get married. Then men have to pretend to be mature and all grown up but secretly they all still enjoy sniffing their farts under the covers.

And, it has been proven in a study by Little Pumpington University, that 82% of all divorces are caused by married men shoving their wives' heads beneath the covers to also appreciate their farts. Ladies do not like this! Ladies, and girls, are just too, well, ladylike to enjoy a good toot of bum gas. BOYS! When you get married, do not shove your wife's head under the duvet to smell your pumps!

Go ask your dad, he'll tell you how bad it can be.

Anyway, as you can imagine, Grandpa Jock dropped one. In truth, he dropped several! A thunderous collection of pooping, parping and pumping had never been heard in the history of flatulence. And only Grandpa Jock was there to enjoy it.

By the time the green smoke had cleared from around Grandpa Jock's head, and the pungent aroma of rotten eggs still lingered in the atmosphere, he found himself

standing onboard a ship, sailing on the high seas, and now surrounded by a dozen grisly pirates, ugly pirates, wearing an assortment of odd clothes...

Yay! We're finally back at the pirate bit again, little reader! Be a bit more patient now, Grandpa Jock hasn't had his head shoved down the cannon yet. Give him a chance, he's only just arrived.

Chapter 9 - Mean
Thursday 15th September 1729

To be honest, Grandpa Jock wasn't really sure if it was the high seas. It might've been the low seas, or just the somewhere-in-the-middle seas. It was all rather watery and the ship was bobbing up and down on the waves, the sun was shining and there were a few tropical islands in the distance; it looked lovely.

What wasn't so lovely were the mean looks of suspicion, surprise, disgust, fear, loathing and greed on the faces of the sailors standing in front of him. They were a scurvy bunch; most of them had teeth missing, many had an eyepatch and all of them had dozens of small scars all over their faces. There were at least two missing hands, replaced by hooks, there was one peg-leg and they were all wearing the oddest assortment of clothes; some were too big, some were too small and some belonged to ladies. There was one pirate wearing a dress and another had a dirty pair of old Y-fronts on his head. Most of them were gripping daggers and one tall, bald pirate at the back was waving a flaming torch. Grandpa Jock backed away as the growling pack of pirates edged towards him, their golden earrings glinting in the sun.

Grandpa Jock inched backwards, trying to squeeze out a little time-travelling trumpet; he didn't care where it took him, just anywhere but here, really. The pirates inched forwards, Grandpa Jock inched backwards, clenching and unclenching his buttocks until he bumped against the large treasure chest behind him. The pirates growled.

'Trying to steal our gold, were ye?' asked the small, fat pirate at the front.

'No, not at all', the old Scotsman replied quickly.

'Well, what's that in yer thievin' little paw?' The pirate pointed at Grandpa Jock's hand with his dagger and he looked down at the gold coin in his palm.

'No...er... this, this is from a bakery,' stammered Grandpa, realising that the evidence looked rather incriminating. His bottom still wasn't playing ball.

'Do you see any bakeries about here?' shouted a tall, thin pirate standing at the back. Grandpa Jock almost burst out laughing when he saw that the tall pirate's hat looked like a pair of an old granny's knickers but now wasn't a good time to laugh.

'Alright, alright, I'm asking the questions,' spat the fat pirate back over his shoulder. 'Do you see any bakeries around here?' he repeated, turning towards Grandpa Jock.

'No, but...' stuttered the old Scotsman, now worried that if he squeezed any harder he would follow through. At least he always went out wearing clean pants, in case he had an accident. But surely he didn't mean this kind of 'accident'.

'He just appeared, Boogly,' gasped a one-eyed pirate.

'From nowhere, Boogly,' agreed another.

'He's a bad omen, Boogly,' moaned One-Eye.

'A curse, I tells ya!' growled Boogly.

The small fat pirate (who was obviously called Boogly) stopped edging forward and stood up tall (well, as tall as you can be when you're only 5foot 2inches tall), turning towards the rest of the crew. 'Would you ladies listen to yourselves?' he shouted, shaking his head. 'We're supposed to be a motley crew of pirates, killers, thieves and vagabonds, and you're all shaking in your little bootees as soon as a baldy old geezer turns up.'

Boogly the pirate turned back to face Grandpa Jock, his

face a little softer beneath the criss-cross of scars. 'Now then old man, I'm guessing you're a stowaway, looking for one last adventure, but it's not good to be messing with pirate gold. These boys will rip you limb from limb... if you're lucky.'

'Honest, sir. I brought this with me. I found it in a bakery!' And Grandpa Jock held up the gold coin in as convincing a manner as he could muster. Boogly ogled the coin. The crew looked at the coin. Grandpa Jock turned the coin round and stared at it.

'That's my George!' he pointed at the heads side.

'Your George?' exclaimed One-Eye.

'That's his face!' gasped Grandpa Jock.

'Who's he and what's his face doing on our treasure?' gawped the tall, thin pirate at the back.

Grandpa Jock had seen the coin lying loose on the floor in the bakery during his first time-warp, and had just enough time to pick it up before he was transported back to his own house. He was still clenching it tightly when he went to bed but he was so dazed he'd forgotten to look at it. Now, he turned the coin over with his fingers. The head on one side definitely looked like George, but he wasn't sure what the tails on the other side meant.

'Erm... yes. See, I told you it was mine. This is my grandson, George,' said Grandpa Jock, trying to ease his way out of another tricky situation.

'So... your grandson has money with his head on it?' One-Eye's one eye narrowed into a suspicious slit. 'Is he a king or sum'fin'?'

'No, no, that's not what I meant,' Grandpa Jock backtracked frantically.

'Let's burn 'im!' shouted the pirate with the torch. Out of the frying pan, into the fire, then back to the frying pan for more curry and into an even hotter fire, thought Grandpa Jock.

'We could hold him for ransom?' yelled the tall pirate with ladies' knickers on his head. 'You know, get some money for him.'

'We're not rich,' squealed the old Scotsman, his moustache jumping wildly up and down. 'I don't know how his head is on here. Maybe it's a special coin.'

'Yeah, but what about all these?' whispered Boogly, opening the treasure chest Grandpa was leaning against with the tip of his dagger. The box was crammed full of coins, jewels and treasure and every one of the golden coins had George's face on one side. Every eye on deck widened in wonder at the glittering prize, two older pirates even began to drool.

CRASH!

Grandpa Jock jumped back with fright, as the lid of the treasure chest slammed shut, snapping Boogly's dagger in half. The rest of the horde cowered back and stared upwards, as Boogly looked angrily at his stumpy little blade.

Standing atop the chest was a mean, enormous pirate, clad in black, with coins woven into his beard and two wide-barrelled pistols in his hands. His eyes were staring wildly, as he growled down at his crew.

'Keep your hands and your hooks off my gold!'

Chapter 10 - Green

Who knows when

 ...ding to legend, leprechauns are tiny, impish creatures, known to hide gold coins in a pot of gold that is hidden at the end of the rainbow. They may be shoemakers, they may make breakfast cereal and they may share their lucky charms with anyone fortunate enough to cross their path.

They may be naughty, mischievous little characters who like to play tricks on humans but if you happen to catch one, he will give you three wishes provided you let him go.

Cobblers!

No, these are myths. Just fairytales and stories told around campfires for hundreds of years, with each generation adding new layers to the legend; softening the truth until leprechauns become cheeky little chaps who dance around with their twinkle-toed little feet and their little buckled shoes and the twiddly-dee, twiddly-dee, twiddly-dee-dee-dee music that follows them everywhere.

Nonsense!

Real leprechauns are greedy. Real leprechauns are nasty. And nasty, greedy, little leprechauns are real!

In this one dark corner of time lived a real leprechaun. There were no bright rainbows here. There were no cute little unicorns skipping around the meadows in this black hovel of a cave. There was just a massive tower of rubber tyres in one corner and a rusty wheelbarrow containing an old cow costume in the other. A big bag of green and gold coloured beans sat underneath the barrow.

And in the centre of the cave stood an enormous black cauldron, rusted around the edges, and propped up on three stumpy legs. The cauldron was empty and the blackness inside was devoid of any light. It was black!

No, I mean it was **BLACK!**

Sometimes black can be mistaken for very, very, very dark blue but in this case, the cauldron was definitely black, and not just dark but a complete absence of light, as if time and space had melted together.

This blackness was a hole. And something was missing from this black hole.

'I beez missing my gold,' growled the little green man, who was standing beside the cauldron, rubbing his hands together.

'And I beez wanting my gold back for sure,' he snarled, and his teeth shone out a golden stream of light from the corner of his mouth.

This wasn't the only light in the cave. Waterfalls trickled down into two inky pools that had formed at the base of the rocks, and in these pools, images rippled.

In the first pool, a bald old Scotsman with a fiery moustache and a flaming fringe of hair around the back of his head could be seen held aloft by a group of pirates. The pirates were forcing the old geezer down the barrel of a cannon head first, and although there was no sound from the pool, there was clearly a great deal of commotion with kicking and wriggling, and a parrot pecking at the heads of the pirates.

The next pool was more of a puddle than a pool, with hardly a drip of water breaking the surface but the image was clearer here. Three children were flying or falling or flapping or fluttering through a green misty cloud.

Time seemed to stand still for them, as they kicked their legs and held their hands together tightly.

'You beez finding my gold,' smirked the little man, a green glow hovering around him. 'You beez fetching that gold for old Tom now.'

And as he watched the pictures and the ripples in the pools, the leprechaun sang to himself…

"Not all my gold does is glitter.
It beez wanting a part of each soul.
And I beez not one to touch it.
Fools enough to inherit that role."

Chapter 11 - Ship Ahoy!

Thursday 15th September 1729

'Who else wants to look at my treasure without permission?' bellowed the huge, black-clad pirate.

'I am the captain around here, and I say when we open that treasure chest!' The coins that were woven into his beard jingled as he shouted, and he waved his two wide-barrelled pistols in the air.

The crew stared down at the deck and shuffled their feet nervously.

'Squawk!' screeched the blue and yellow parrot on the Captain's shoulder. 'Pieces of eight! Pieces of eight!' and the parrot lifted his tail and fluffed up his feathers. Dollop after dollop of poop plopped out of its bottom.

Grandpa Jock was sitting opposite the small, fat pirate on the deck. The watery white poop splattered all over Boogly's head and ran down the side of his face. Splodge, splodge, splodge.

'What have you been feeding that blasted bird?!' Boogly yelled as he jumped to his feet. 'You'll pay for breaking my favourite blade.'

'Yaaarrrr! So you have some spirit in you, Boogly,' growled the Captain. He was smiling now but not in a nice way, like a shark swimming up to a seal. 'Maybe you'd like to taste one of my cats?'

'Oooooooh,' cooed the crew, shuffling further away from the chubby, little pirate, leaving Boogly standing alone and isolated.

'I'm not scared of you or your catapults,' Boogly argued. 'This is the worst pirate ship I've ever sailed on.'

'But what about this treasure then? A pretty pile of gold, if I do say so. Eh, lads?' laughed the Captain and crew joined in with a rousing cheer.

'Yaaarrrr!' they shouted.

'Yarr my butt,' grumbled Boogly. 'You found that treasure by mistake. We didn't steal it. We didn't plunder it or rob it. You stumbled over it!'

'*Catapult, catapult!*' screeched the parrot.

'Catapult indeed, Wilberforce,' sang the Captain, glowering now. 'No one challenges Captain Jack and gets away with it. As Mr Boogly is about to find out.' He raised one of his pistols and aimed at the small fat pirate. Boogly gulped, his short-lived courage draining out of the bottom of his britches in a puddle.

There was a loud bang and a puff of smoke. The pistol recoiled, as a small ginger cat exploded out of the barrel and shot towards Boogly. As it flew through the air the cat twisted and turned until it was pointing towards the terrified pirate, claws first, and landed squarely on Boogly's face.

In a flurry of fur and parrot poop, the small cat unleashed its fury all at once, sharp little claws and teeth taking out their vengeance on the first thing it saw. Boogly tried to grab at the cat but this only served to make it madder; pulling it off his face would've resulted in more scars and a lot more blood. Wisps of smoke were curling up from the cat's ears and patches of its fur were singed and blackened.

Once the cat had tired itself out clawing at Boogly, it jumped off his head and hopped up onto the upper deck to lick the blood and parrot poop from its fur. Boogly sat in a wasted heap in the corner.

'That's what happens when you mess with Captain Jack Parrott,' announced the captain, as he glowered around the rest of his crew.

Grandpa Jock just stared at Captain Jack Parrott, who was now standing proudly on top of the treasure chest and blowing the smoke from the barrel of his cat-gun. Wilberforce the parrot nuzzled into the pirate's beard and picked the fleas from his hair.

'SHIP AHOY!' came a voice from up in the crow's nest, and Wilberforce the parrot flew up to a high vantage point on the rigging. The crew turned together and ran to the balustrade. On the horizon Grandpa Jock could barely make out the black silhouette of a large sailing ship but the pirates were becoming excited.

'Roll out the guns, lads,' shouted Captain Jack, as he loaded another kitten into his pistol. The little cat meowed, as it was squeezed into the barrel and covered in gunpowder. Grandpa Jock was sure he'd heard a small *atishoo* coming from inside the gun. Captain Jack holstered his pistol and strode over to the gun deck to bark his orders. Grandpa Jock tried to melt into the treasure chest, staying as quiet and unseen as possible.

He peeked his head out gingerly and saw Captain Jack grab the collars of the blouses of Tall-Bald and One-Eye, pulling their heads together and whispering into their ears. Both pirates glanced back at the treasure chest and then ran towards the old Scotsman. Grandpa Jock pressed himself into the corner but he knew it was useless.

Tall-Bald picked up a rope from the deck, as One-Eye grabbed Grandpa Jock's ankle and dragged him out onto the deck. Grandpa Jock felt a little bit of wee leaking out into his pants as he struggled to free himself from the pirate's grasp, until One-Eye planked himself down on his chest. The pirate's bottom was inches from Grandpa Jock's face and the smell could not be described as pleasant.

Grandpa Jock stopped wriggling, as Tall-Bald wrapped the ropes tightly around his legs. Next his hands were tied and the two pirates hauled the old geezer up onto his feet and thrust him head first into the largest cannon on the top deck, careless enough to bang his head against the rim on the way in.

'But what if we needs to fire this 'un?' The voice was muffled and echoey. Maybe it was Tall-Bald, Grandpa Jock couldn't be sure, his head was too woozy.

'Well, the old fella will quickly learn how to fly, won't he!' chuckled One-Eye, the voices growing fainter, as a blanket of stars wrapped softly around Grandpa Jock's head. Maybe he passed out, maybe the cannon just grew darker but either way, Grandpa Jock was sure he would throw up.

Peck, peck, peck, then POP!

'Aaawwkk!' croaked the parrot.

'Well, excuse me, sir. I wish to remove myself from this stinking ship as much as you do but getting yourself captured again will not help either of us, will it?' said the parrot.

'You just spoke?' spluttered Grandpa Jock.

'Of course I just spoke. All parrots can speak!' replied the parrot.

'Yes but... but usually just, like, parrot-fashion.' Grandpa Jock stumbled over his words. 'I mean, just repeating phrases... *Polly wants a cracker*... and stuff like that.'

'As I said, all parrots can talk. We're just rather fussy who we talk to,' declared the bird, puffing out the feathers on its chest.

Chapter 12 - Who?

Present day

By now, little reader, you will have noticed that the timeline of this story has been jumping around recently. Once the magic beans were unleashed, we read about Grandpa Jock's head being stuck in a cannon and freed by the parrot in Chapter 7.

Then, we leapt back to the night before and his bedtime bottom burps in Chapter 8 before we zoomed forward to the start of his pirate adventure in Chapter 9. Finally, we discovered how his head ended up in the cannon in Chapter 11, and then we found out that the parrot's name was Wilberforce.

And in between all that, Tiny Tom the Leprechaun has had two little chapters all to himself.

This is called a non-linear narrative.

Oo-ooh! Fancy-nancy!

It is a story telling technique sometimes used in books, films and television, where events are shown out of their proper order, and the story does not follow a direct pattern. It often mimics the structure and recall of human memory.

Wow, how educational is this?!

Sometimes it shows two parallel plot lines, or dream sequences or flashbacks, or flash-forwards, or in this case, the confusion of time-travel. It can also be a narrative hook, which grips the reader and shouts 'Keep reading! You'll find out later.'

And that's because time is not a straight line. It doesn't always go forward; it loops and swoops and poops and pops out to the shops and meets itself coming back again. It's a big bag of wibbly-wobbly, timey-wimey sort of stuff, as some other old time-traveller said... I can't remember Who.

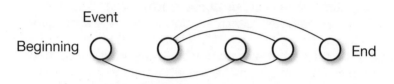

Reader-defined Pathway

And it also means you are becoming smarter, as a little reader, in joining the dots, making the inter-connections and just plain better at understanding multiple storylines.

You little smarty-pants, you.

So what are you waiting around here for? Keep reading, butt-face!

Chapter 13 - Wonderland

The world that they knew began to disappear. George, Kenny and Allison could not stop themselves from falling through time. It was like dropping down a very deep well.

Either the well was very deep, or they fell very slowly, for they had plenty of time as they went down to look about and to wonder what was going to happen next. First, they tried to look down and make out what they were coming to, but it was too dark to see anything. Then they looked at the sides of the well, and noticed that they were filled with calendars and maps hung upon pegs. The three of them still held tightly onto each other.

Down, down, down. Would the fall NEVER come to an end!

'I wonder how many miles we've fallen?' Kenny said aloud. 'We must be at least four thousand miles down.'

'We're not falling *down*, Kenny. We're falling *through*,' insisted George. 'Through time, so it will be years, not miles.'

'Was it like this the last time you warped away?' Allison was usually a step or two ahead of the boys, and George realised that his last journey felt much shorter.

'Maybe we're heavier... because there's three of us this time,' answered George, still completely in the dark in more ways than one.

'Or maybe we're not falling down at all,' pondered Allison. 'Maybe we're falling forwards. Or backwards in time, or into the future even.'

George stared at her in amazement. Once, not so long ago, when they first met, George had called her *Allison Wonderland*, since her imagination was able to dream up the most far-fetched fairy stories he'd ever heard. Now, he realised, she may just have a point this time.

Down, down, down. Or up, up, up. Or through, through, through, depending on their point of view. There was nothing else to do, so Allison began talking again.

'Do you think there will be cats in the future?' she wondered aloud. The boys just stared at her again, not quite sure how to reply. 'Cats with opposable thumbs,' she continued. 'Cats with opposable thumbs would be smart enough to take over the world. They'd make us their slaves.'

Allison pulled her hand away from Kenny and wiggled her thumb at George. 'See, opposable thumbs.'

'It's really dark in here,' said Kenny, trying to change the subject. 'Do you think there are bats?'

'Do cats eat bats?' asked Allison.

'Or, more worryingly, do bats eat cats?' George added, when suddenly, thump! thump! thump! down they came upon the deck of galleon, and their fall through time was over.

Well, not quite over. Kenny landed on the deck of the galleon but George and Allison were nowhere to be seen. The moment that Allison pulled her hand away to show George her opposable thumb, she also broke the timeline and Kenny dropped slightly faster into the void.

Which meant he arrived sooner, much sooner, than his two friends.

'Alright, wee man. How are you doing?' asked a familiar

voice. Kenny turned, and saw Grandpa Jock crouched behind a large chest.

'Mister Jock! You're here!' cried Kenny, who then paused. 'But where's here?'

'Not just where, lad. When's here?' Grandpa Jock nodded wisely and his bushy eyebrows knitted together.

'Well, if you really must know, young man, the year is 1729 and you are on board the pirate ship known as The Jammy Roger, captained by that hopeless Jack Parrott and sailing course towards the Cayman Islands, to the west of the Caribbean,' nodded the blue and yellow bird sitting on the chest behind Grandpa Jock.

'That's Wilberforce,' added Grandpa Jock. 'He's a parrot.'

'I can see that, Mr Jock,' spluttered Kenny. 'But I thought they just repeated things. He's actually having a conversation... I thought that was impossible.'

'Young man, everything always seems impossible until it's done,' the parrot continued. 'So many of our dreams at first seem impossible, then they seem improbable, and then, when we summon the will, they soon become inevitable. Sometimes I've believed as many as six impossible things before breakfast.'

'He's quite a talker, isn't he?' giggled Kenny.

'You do not need to discuss me in the third person, young man, when I am clearly sitting in front of you. That is the height of rudeness,' Wilberforce went on. 'The golden age of piracy is certainly drawing to a close and... watch out for the cat poo.'

Kenny felt the squelch as he leaned back and placed his hand on the deck. Brown mush oozed between his fingers and he yakked.

'Urgh, it's all over my hand,' groaned Kenny, as he tried to wipe the muck off his fingers, scraping each one across the deck.

'You really must watch out for these things,' said Wilberforce. 'We are faced with truly horrible conditions on board ship these days. It used to be the age of exploration and adventure but now... Cat poo!'

Both Kenny and Grandpa Jock lifted up their hands.

'Cat poo.' Wilberforce pointed with his wing towards another little brown parcel.

'That's probably why they call this bit of a ship the poop deck,' laughed Grandpa Jock

'More cat poo, over there.' Wilberforce pointed to his left this time.

'Cat poo.'

Cat poo.'

'Rat poo.'

'Cat poo.' And Wilberforce finally stopped pointing to the deck.

'Bat poo?' asked Kenny helpfully.

'Don't be stupid, boy. We are on board a ship one hundred nautical miles from land. There are no bats on board ship.'

'He's quite touchy, isn't he?' whispered Kenny.

'I also have excellent hearing, young man,' said the parrot, fluffing up his feather. 'And you'd be touchy too, if you had to keep plucking lice and fleas and maggots out of your feathers. Honestly, the hygiene standards of these scoundrels is simply shocking.'

Grandpa Jock sat up sharply. 'But Kenny, if you're here, and I've been here for hours, then...'

'...Where are George and Allison?'

Chapter 14 - Tea

Thursday 15th September 1729

Of course, as soon as Allison released Kenny's hand, she created an alternative time-loop. Kenny arrived on board the pirate ship first, and although George and Allison were a split second behind him, they arrived two hours later.

In the middle of the battle!

Several pages previously, someone shouted 'SHIP AHOY!' from the crow's nest high above the galleon, just as the black silhouette of a large ship was sailing into view.

'Roll out the guns, lads,' shouted Captain Jack, and the crew leapt into action. They rolled out the guns, they rolled out the barrels, they stoked gun powder into their cannons and prepared to fire.

Some of the motley crew unpacked wooden boxes filled with swords and pistols from the cargo nets that were stacked at one end of the ship. Other crew members opened the hatches below decks and rolled out even more cannons.

The ships sailed closer and the crew readied their positions. Unfortunately, on a clear day in the Caribbean, when the sky is bright and the sea shimmers golden green and sapphire blue, ships can be spotted miles away. And galleons are not exactly fast, with even the swiftest ship reaching only 8 knots; that's about the speed of a fast jogger.

So it was taking ages for the ships to come together. The adrenalin and the excitement and the nervous energy of the pirates had burned off quickly and many of them were becoming bored now. Some sat on the barrels of their cannons.

Some picked the insect larvae out of their beards and others picked at their noses with the tips of their cutlasses.

'We could do with some tea, boss,' shouted Boogly, his bravery slowly returning. 'You know, keep us on our toes.'

'TEA?' screamed the captain. 'TEA! You're meant to be pirates! You should be drinking RUM!'

'Well, sorry boss. None of the lads actually like rum, sir,' Boogly shuffled. 'We only drinks it cos it's the done thing. We'd all prefer a nice cup of tea, really.'

It was then that Grandpa Jock noticed the tall, thin pirate sneak off to the far side of the ship, where he sat down in the corner and began to cry. His chiseled face was covered in tiny scars and pockmarks, and the tears ran down his uneven cheeks. Then he pulled out a delicate handkerchief from the pocket in his breeches and gave his nose a satisfying blast. Not everyone on board was a brave and bloodthirsty buccaneer.

Captain Jack Parrott heard this raspberry toot too, and jumped off the upper deck, leapt over the cargo nets and stood above the whimpering pirate.

'Are you a coward or a cutthroat?' bellowed the captain, pulling out both of his wide-barrel pistols and aiming them at the tall, thin pirate, who was still wearing his frilly granny-knickers hat. Both pistols miaowed softly.

'Do you want another taste of cat-apult?' said Captain Jack. The scars on the pirate's face was a clear demonstration that he'd been mauled by the moggies many times before, perhaps each time he'd lost his nerve before battle. 'Maybe both barrels this time… a pair of plundering pussy-cats to pluck out yer eyes.'

The quivering pirate threw his arms up around his head and whimpered.

'Y'aaaarrr,' roared the captain, 'Get out of my sight, ya scurvy dog. Go below deck and make the crew their brew.'

Now, everyone likes a nice cup of tea. And everyone knows that a tea-bag is a light, delicate little object. But 10,000 teabags altogether weigh the exact same amount as your average ten-year old child. Therefore, two ten-year old children holding hands are obviously the same weight as 20,000 teabags. And the mass of 20,000 teabags travelling at a terminal velocity of 120 miles per hour would hit a person (or pirate) with the energy of a small charging elephant.

Captain Jack Parrott had seen an elephant once, when he was pirating off the coast of north Africa. He was onboard a ship and the elephant was standing on a beach so technically, he had never been struck by an elephant. But that is what it felt like when two children dropped out of the sky and landed on his head.

They knocked him flat!

The children stood up, slightly dazed but completely unhurt. There might not be any gravity in time-travel but the landings can suck!

Captain Parrott however, dropped his cat-pistols to the side and crumpled up in a ball next to the crying pirate with lady's pants on his head.

Definitely not a normal day, thought George.

But he didn't have long to think because Boogly the pirate had been watching his captain with great interest (hoping for the cup of tea he'd asked for) and when he spotted his chance to regain favour with his captain, he jumped at it. Clambering up the rigging to the top mast, he slashed at a guy rope with his cutlass and the jigger sail at the back of the ship jolted. The mizzen mast dropped, whilst cogs and gears whizzed. Ropes tightened and the counterweights pulled sharply downwards.

Counterweights on a ship are used with a block and tackle pulley system to hoist cargo onboard and unload cargo in port. Unfortunately, George and Allison were standing on top of the galleon's largest cargo net, which was lying spread out on the deck. As the counterweights went down, the net (and the children) went shooting upwards.

George and Allison were now dangling high above the pirate ship, looking down, with a great view of the decks below. They could see a dozen pirates running to and fro, mainly in a panicking attempt to look busy, and a large pirate clad in black staggering to his feet angrily. They could see a tall, thin pirate with frilly underpants on his head rushing towards the galley hatch and they spied a blur of ginger hair (and a small bald head) with a flurry of blue and yellow feathers besides a large treasure chest.

The blue and yellow blur fluttered upwards.

And on the bow of the ship, at the very prow of the front was the figurehead. George knew that these mascots were usually carved from wood, and often painted gold, and although this figurehead had a slight golden glitter about its face, he thought it strange that its body was painted black and white. It seemingly depicted a bull.

In all the confusion, the other ship had turned tail and was now sailing away from the pirates without even a shot being fired, and the pirates were becoming agitated that they were missing out on the prize. Captain Parrott had climbed up on top of the cargo boxes and was barking new orders to his crew, who were rushing around with a clearer purpose this time.

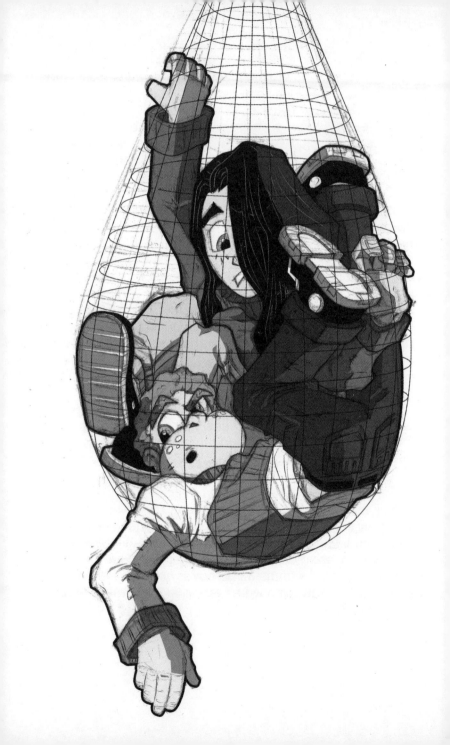

Now, to be struck by the weight of a small charging elephant once may be considered unfortunate but to be smashed twice on the same day is just downright carelessness.

Captain Jack Parrott was flattened completely again, as the cargo net dropped from above. Wilberforce had flown up to the top rigging and had pecked through the ropes holding the net in place, and the cargo bag, and Allison and George dropped heavily.

'If you two young whipper-snappers would oblige me by moving your little butts in a brisker fashion, I would very much like to depart this vessel,' ordered the parrot, as he fluttered around their heads.

'Over here!' yelled Grandpa Jock, from up on the poop deck, and George and Allison started towards the stairs.

'Grab his pistols,' squawked Wilberforce, and Allison stopped to pick up the two enormously wide-barrelled flintlocks before racing up the steps.

'Grab that treasure chest,' shouted the ship's cow-like mascot, who had mysteriously moved from the front of the boat around to the stern, in a blur of bovine brilliance.

As relieved as they all were to see each other again, there was no time for greetings. The pirates had spotted what was going on, and even without the orders of their captain, who was still lying flat out on the deck below, they were closing in again.

'Here,' shouted George. 'Swallow one of these and hold on!' And he pulled out a small handful of dried beans from his pocket and held them out.

'But they're raw,' cried Grandpa Jock. 'We've no idea how they'll work.'

'I don't think we have much choice, Grandpa.'

George, Kenny, Allison and Grandpa Jock each took a bean and knocked them back with swift slug, swallowing them whole without even chewing.

The pirates had reached the top of the stairs and were now inching forward, cutlasses, daggers and pistols drawn. They growled, they hissed and they snarled, drawing energy from each other and becoming braver by the second because they were part of a bigger gang (most bullies are like this).

And as the pirates inched forwards, our gang inched backwards, clenching and unclenching their buttocks, hoping for some sort of release.

Grandpa Jock was first to unleash his bottom blast. Thunderous ripples shuddered down his legs and George grabbed his hand for support. At that point, George let one out too.

Immediately, Kenny and Allison were also gripped by their own enormous explosions, as Crayon held onto the large wooden chest beside him to keep his balance. With two pirate pistols in one hand, Allison could only grab hold of Kenny's arm with the other.

'Squawk!' screeched the parrot.

'Screech!' squawked Kenny, as Wilberforce dug his claws into the boy's shoulder. Kenny grimaced in pain but the parrot refused to let go.

Green mists swirled around them and the blackness came calling.

'Let's do the time-warp again,' laughed Grandpa Jock, as all five time-travellers were drawn into the vortex.

Chapter 15 - Wee

Present day

Of course, you may have spotted this already, for I know that you are a smart little reader but there were not just five time-travellers in the vortex.

No, there were seven.

Hi-ho!
Seven little travellers, off in time they go.
Where they will land, no one can know.
Give them some beans, and watch them blow.
Hi-ho! Hi-ho! Hi-ho!

Ahem...

Sorry about that, little reader. I was starting to sound a bit like that nasty, little leprechaun, wasn't I? It's frightening how easily people can become attracted to the dark side. Don't go there!
But I digress.
Do you know who the extra two time-travellers are?
No, well I'm not telling you.

MMMMWAAHAHAHAHAHAHAHAHAHAHA!

(Sorry again, little reader, I didn't really need to add that last bit. I just wanted to write mwahahaha and say it out loud in a scary voice as I was typing.)

(To be honest, I scared myself too.)
(Luckily, no wee came out.)

Chapter 16 - Home Alone

Present day

As the smoke drifted away, a blue and yellow bird coughed, spluttered and cleared its throat. It wiped its beak on its feathers, snuffled and looked around.

The room was a curious collection of old and new. On the wall there was a painting of a magnificent stag on the side of a mountain, which Wilberforce presumed to be in Scotland. At one side of the mantelpiece was an old wooden clock that ticked noisily, whilst at the other side was a stack of video games.

The armchair that sat directly in front of the television was ancient, burst and battered, and held together with duct tape. The TV, on the other hand, was absolutely enormous, almost filling the whole wall that it was mounted on, and underneath it sat a Playstation4, and Xbox One and a Nintendo Switch.

'Well, it wouldn't hurt to redecorate occasionally,' sniffed Wilberforce. 'That wallpaper is positively nineteenth century.'

'We're back in Grandpa Jock's house,' whispered Allison, waving her hand in front of her face to clear the smoke.

'And that armchair is only good enough for the dump,' the parrot went on.

'Hey! Mr Jock loves that chair. He says it's a snug fit for his bottom,' argued Kenny. 'And we just rescued you from that stinking pirate ship and I have the scars to prove it.' Kenny pulled his t-shirt down over his shoulder to reveal three livid red scratches.

'And that wasn't exactly the lap of luxury, so a little more gratitude would be appreciated,' added Allison, not quite . realising that she was arguing with a parrot.

'And where did George and Mr Jock go?' asked Kenny, looking around.

'Miaow'

'And where did this trunk come from?' asked Allison, tapping the wooden box with her hand.

'Miaow'

'And why has nobody offered me a cracker yet? That always happens when I meet new people and I am rather peckish,' laughed Wilberforce, trying to sound cheerier.

'Miaow'

'Peckish. Get it,' chuckled the parrot again. 'With my beak. Peckish.'

Nobody laughed.

'Miaow'

'And who keeps saying 'Miaow?' cried Kenny, scratching his head and no longer listening to the parrot.

Allison dropped down behind the wooden chest and picked up the two wide-barrelled pirate pistols she had brought back through the time-warp. She set them down gently on top of the chest and started looking for a latch or a catch or any other way to open them. Her finger caught hold of a lever just above the grip and both barrels snapped open, exposing the breech ends.

And a small, ginger kitten crawled out. Its dark eyes were huge, its ears were pulled back timidly and the frightened little cat crawled out of the gun and looked around meekly.

'*Felix pistolium bombarda,*' mused Wilberforce, his wings tucked behind his back. 'Otherwise know as a cat-apult.'

'You're making that up,' snarled Kenny,

'Choose not to believe it if you wish but trust me, that is a cat-apult,' nodded the bird. 'And I have seen enough of them to last me a lifetime.'

'How would you know that?' asked Kenny angrily. 'You're just a parrot.'

'That is true,' nodded the parrot. 'Although perhaps not just a parrot. I am a very, very, very old bird indeed. I have seen a great many things in my long life-time and many of these things I would prefer not to remember.'

'It is a little-known fact,' the parrot went on, 'that towards the end of the golden age of piracy, when proper ammunition was scarce, some pirates would use live cats to fire into the faces of their enemies. These little beasts were so furious at being fired out of a pistol at high-speed that they would claw and scratch anything they landed upon, giving the shooter a massive advantage. Hence, the cat-apult.'

Kenny was beginning to wish he hadn't insulted the bird because once the parrot started talking there was no stopping him.

'I am Wilberforce, by the way. We haven't been introduced.' The parrot was now addressing Allison but she wasn't listening. She was too busy playing with the little ball of fluff that crawled out of the pistol.

'Aawww, look at you,' she crooned. 'You're soooo cute. You're so fluffy. You're so huggable. Oh, I love you, I love your little feet, I love your little nose…' The kitten had rolled over onto its side and was gently patting her fingers with one of its paws.

"That's Allison, by the way,' said Kenny to Wilberforce, rolling his eyes. 'She might be some time.'

'That is quite all right, young man,' said the parrot. 'I fully understand the attraction of adorable cuteness to young ladies. The sweetness and innocence of teddy bears, unicorns, small animals and basically any little ball of fluff with large eyes have always maintained a lovable charm for girls. They are hard-wired that way, they… erm… I would not touch that, if I were you, Kenneth.'

Crayon Kenny's mind was a melting pot of ideas and

imagination, but he had the attention span of a small hamster. Halfway through Wilberforce's speech about the allure of cute little balls of fur Kenny had drifted off towards the wooden chest and was poking at the large pistol. The two barrels ran parallel, side by side, with a pair of wide mouths at the far end.

Kenny picked up the gun and it snapped shut, closing the barrels tight against the grip and the trigger mechanism. He turned it around in his hands, feeling the weight and pointing it towards the living room wall.

'That is really a rather dreadful idea, young man,' said the parrot, covering its face with one wing. 'It may be...'

BANG!

'...loaded.'

The pistol exploded. Or at least, one end of the pistol exploded and a bright orange flash shot through the room. The bright orange fluffy flash squealed as it flew through the air and landed with a SPLAT! on the wall, legs outstretched in four different directions, its tail smoking.

'Now would be a good time for us to leave the room,' insisted Wilberforce, as the still smouldering kitten slid down the wall, stopped, turned, pounced and landed on its feet. The vicious little fur-ball glared around the room, eyes burning and claws scratching at the carpet. Kenny, Allison and Wilberforce backed themselves into the kitchen and quickly closed the door.

*

Well, little reader, I just wanted to share something with you. Two of the words I used on that last page were BANG! and SPLAT!

These are good examples of ONOMATOPOEIA. Go on, try saying that one.

Oh - no - ma - toe - pee - ah

When the name of an action imitates the sound it makes, it's known as an onomatopoeia, like bang, or splat, or thump, or thud, or pop, or plop.

The noises that animals and birds make can also be called onomatopoeia.

Dogs bark, cats miaow, parrots squawk, bees buzz, cows moo and snakes hiss. Can you think of any more?

And it's such a cool word too, with twelve letters in it. Eight of them are vowels and only four consonants. If you can learn to say it, and slip it into conversation, people will think you're a genius!

Anyway, back to the action.

*

'What do we do now?' squealed Kenny, as the crashing, slashing and screeching on the other side of the door grew louder and louder.

'Technically, one of us needs to go back in there and soothe the animal,' said Wilberforce. 'You know, calm it down.'

'You can go in, Allison. You're good with animals.'

'Why me?' replied Allison. 'You're the muppet who fired that stupid gun.'

'I didn't know it was going to go off,' complained Kenny, trying to defend the undefensible.

'What did you think it was going to do? Blow raspberries!' Allison was stroking the other little kitten, who was quite happily resting in her hands, purring gently.

'Okay, okay. I'll do it,' agreed Kenny, as the noise levels in the living began to calm down. 'Make way for Mr Superhero!'

And Kenny pushed passed Allison and Wilberforce and slowly opened the door.

Chapter 17 - Toes

Present day - I think

A large puddle of water slopped around the floor of the cave, as a small pantomime cow crawled out of the larger pool of water by the wall.

The cow costume was actually designed for two people to wear together and the current wearer of the outfit could only really be described as half a person, since he was less than one metre tall. Hooves splashed on the floor and the cow's head dropped off into the much smaller pool, or puddle, if you'd prefer. It was actually a disgrace of a pool, if the truth be told.

'It beez a disgrace,' muttered the leprechaun, pulling down his cow trousers, revealing his green suit. He had only worn one pair, and the other set sat in a heap beneath the black cauldron in the corner. 'They needz a-poking and a-prodding and a-pushing all the time,' grunted Tiny Tom to himself. 'They beez looking in all the wrong places without Tom's help.'

'And it beez my gold after all, Tom's gold, nobody else's,' he muttered again. 'Mine, all mine, collected over thousands of years… and youz lost it.' And the little leprechaun aimed a kick at the cauldron.

Of course, the cauldron didn't mind being kicked. It was just a cauldron, made of iron, squat and black and sitting on three little legs. It had no feelings, it had no personality and it didn't have a soul.

But Tiny Tom the Leprechaun had feelings, and at that precise moment, he felt his toes crumple as his shoe made contact with the side of the cauldron. One unstoppable force meeting one immovable object. But the unstoppable force did stop, quite suddenly, when Tom felt his tiny toe bones crunch and he let out a howl of pain and anger and frustration.

The leprechaun hopped around the cave clutching his foot, yelping in agony, as his crumpled toes seemed to burn, and he cursed his luck. And all the lucky charms in his world were useless in finding the gold, so scattered across history it was.

But his magic beans… they knew where the gold was. And all he needed were one or two greedy fools to help him.

Tom sat down beside the larger pool now, and rubbed his toes gently, water flowing down the wall of the cave behind him. The surface of the pool was quite still and colour began to shimmer across it like reflections dancing on glass.

'The boy and the old fool, together again.
With no idea where, and no idea when.
The beanz chooze the flowing,
And the going and the knowing.
And when I gets my gold, what then? What then?'

The little man drummed his fingers together, watching the scenes unfold on the water, his teeth glinting with every shimmer and ripple of light, and he sniggered continually.

'Every piece of gold that they touch,
Absorbs their souls a little too much.
I won't touch it. I won't dare.
But if they turn bad, I won't care.'

Chapter 18 - A Big Bang Theory

Throughout Time

The whole universe was in a hot, dense state.
Then nearly 14 billion years ago, time starts to inflate.

The gold began to cool, the dinosaurs began to drool.
Neanderthals developed tools.

They climbed a wall (they climbed the pyramids)
Math, science, history, all warping in the mysteries
That all started with a bottom burp.

Bang!

NO TECHNOLOGY OR ROCKETRY

Just bum-blasting Grandpa Jocketry...

...and their functions came out bodily...

...with force and high velocity...

...and the occasional apology...

Chapter 19 - A Cheeky Cheesy Chapter

Present day

What a marvellous montage of comical cartoons and a cool collection of characters.
Throughout this book, little reader, you will have noticed that I like to use words that start with the same sound in the same sentence.
This is a called an alliteration. I LOVE ALLITERATIONS where some of the words start with the same sound in the same sentence - S-S-S-S-S-S-S.

Big bottom burps!

That's probably my favourite alliteration of all. Or yearning to be young and youthful - that's me really. I don't want to be old. Like Grandpa Jock, I want to be young again. Time always flows forwards, but I wish time could bend backwards.

All my book titles are alliterations too: Giant Geriatric Generator, Zigzag Zit-faced Zombies, Unidentified Unsinkable Underpants, Jumbo Jobby Juicer, Stupid Stinky Stories - all words that start with the same sound, and not words you would expect to see together in the same sentence - to me, they conjure up a crazy creative concept in my cranium.

Continue, kids...

Chapter 20 - Physics

Present day

'Honestly Kenny,' groaned Allison. 'I have never heard a superhero scream as much as you. Super - no! Hero - definitely not.' And she finished putting the last adhesive plaster onto the side of his face. He wore several.

'It was hideous,' wept Kenny. 'An evil ball of fur and fangs and claws. I was lucky to get out there alive.'

'Well, if you ask me,' said Wilberforce, 'I've never seen a superhero wet their pants before. And I would think it would be rather obvious, since superheroes wear their pants on the outside of the costumes.'

'Well, nobody asked you,' groaned Kenny. 'And I didn't wet myself. I… erm… knocked over a cold cup of tea that was next to Mr Jock's chair.'

'And how could you say this little ball of fluff is evil,' crooned Allison, as she tickled both kittens under their chins. 'They're both too cute… coochy, coochy coo.'

The cats were both sitting contentedly on the sofa, the second kitten having calmed down from the unexpected launching from the pistol. Kenny had entered the living room just as the last explosive energy was seeping from the frightened little animal but he tasted just enough to understand why cat-apults were such a valuable weapon.

Now the kittens were purring softly. Allison smoothed their fur and they both wrinkled their little noses up against her hand, as she fluffed her fingers behind their ears.

'I'm going to call you Mr Snuffles,' whispered Allison softly. 'And I'm going to call you…'

'SPLAT!' shouted Kenny. 'Call that one Splat! There are two kittens so we should each choose a name… and I'm calling that one Splat!'

'You can't call a kitten Splat,' replied Allison, turning her nose up.

'Yes, it's called Splat!,' decided Kenny. 'Splat! with an exclamation mark at the end. That's how you have to spell it, so when you send him a birthday card you have to remember to add the exclamation mark!'

'Splat the Cat,' said Allison. 'Why Splat?'

'Don't forget the exclamation mark!'

'But why Splat!?' asked Allison.

'So I can remember what that vicious little monster looked like when he hit the wall,' laughed Kenny, and he turned to Wilberforce to enjoy the joke.

'Have you never heard of karma, Kenneth?' the parrot asked, bowing his head to the side. 'Karma is basically *Do good things, and good things happen. Do bad things and you'd better watch out*. Nobody should ever want to hurt a little cat. Or a dog or any animal, or person. Do bad things Kenneth, and karma will find you and bite you on the bottom.'

'I didn't mean any harm,' said Kenny, sheepishly, 'but I'm the one covered in plasters here.'

Wilberforce shook his head, tutted quietly and fluffed up his feathers. He was now sitting on top of the wooden chest, pecking at the padlock with the tip of his beak. He realised that both Kenny and Allison were staring at him but he carried on pecking until the lock gave out a satisfying click and the chest popped open. It was filled with hundreds of gold coins.

'As I expected,' nodded Wilberforce, too smart for his own good. 'We seem to have acquired some pirate gold.'

The whole room glittered with the light from the treasure, glinting and sparkling and shining a thousand little golden beams around the walls. Kenny leaned forward, staring at the coins

'Does that look like George?' Kenny nodded towards a coin on top of the pile. 'On that one… oops, and that one too. And that one.' Kenny gasped, pointing at the whole pile. 'They're *all* George!'

The entire chest was filled with golden coins with George's face on one side, and the bottom of an animal on the other.

'Definitely heads or tails,' chuckled Kenny. 'George's head and a cow's tail. Or a camel, or it might be a horse's bottom.'

Allison had forgotten about the cats for a moment, and moved closer, peering into the chest and reaching out her hand.

'It's best not to touch them,' said Wilberforce, aiming a peck at her fingers.

'Ow,' cried Allison, pulling her hand away quickly. 'Why not?'

'When you reach the same age as I am, young lady, you will hopefully have learned a little bit about the world.' Wilberforce was fluffing up his feathers again, with his usual air of self-importance.

'And many years ago, I learned about gold.'

'How much is there to know about gold?' spluttered Kenny. 'It's metal, it's yellow, it's shiny and that's about it.'

'There's a little more to it than that, boy,' nodded the bird, and Kenny dropped his head. He hated being called 'boy' like that but he hated even more starting the parrot off again. Allison leaned in closer.

'The chemical symbol for gold is Au, from the Greek word *aurum*, which means glow of sunshine,' declared Wilberforce. 'The English word gold comes from the words gulb and ghel also referring to the colour. It is the only metal of this colour ever known.'

'Gold's characteristic yellow colour is due to the

arrangement of its electrons and the secret lies in its atomic structure,' said the parrot. 'Quantum mechanics doesn't even begin to explain it.'

Even Kenny was leaning in closer now.

'Golden atoms are so heavy and the electrons move so fast that you now have to include Albert Einstein's theory of relativity into the maths.' And Wilberforce beckoned them in closer with his wing.

'It is only when you fold together quantum mechanics with relativity that suddenly you understand it.'

Allison looked at Kenny, and Kenny stared at Allison and neither of them knew what the parrot was talking about but he spoke with so much confidence that they just had to believe him.

'Every other metal, in their purest forms, reflect light straight back out,' said Wilberforce, speaking slower now, hoping the kids were keeping up. 'But gold electrons slosh around quickly and this means that gold absorbs a bit of the blue spectrum light. That's why the light reflected back is a distinctive golden colour.'

'And if you believe the legends,' whispered Wilberforce, 'Gold even absorbs your soul...'

DUN, DUN, DUN!

'Hang on, hang on,' snapped Allison. 'I was kinda getting the chemistry part, and I know a bit about electrons and protons and atoms and stuff. But absorbing your soul? No chance.'

'Er, what? I mean, yeah, yeah, what she said,' spluttered Kenny, still trying to remember who Albert Einstein was. 'No chance!'

Wilberforce looked a little crest-fallen. His plumage

drooped and his tail slumped between his legs. Nobody had ever questioned his tales before. The pirates had always believed his stories, no questions asked, but faced with two cynical ten year olds he was stumped.

'Well, they are legends after all,' backtracked the parrot. 'And even the Aztecs called gold the "excrement of the gods".'

'What's excrement?' whispered Kenny.

'It's another word for poo,' whispered Allison.

'God Poo?' barfed Kenny. 'No wonder gold can absorb your soul.'

'Look, it's just an ancient legend,' argued the parrot. 'I haven't exactly seen it with my own eyes but I have seen gold make people do strange things. Bad things, evil things sometimes; it taints people; makes them greedy.'

'Okay,' agreed Allison. 'That I can understand, and for your sake, we won't touch this stuff yet.' Kenny looked disappointed. 'But I want to know exactly what we're dealing with here.'

'I'm afraid I don't follow you, young lady,' said the parrot.

'We need to go to the museum!' replied Allison.

A quick note to the little readers here - Chapter 21 may be rather yucky. It's not my fault, it's just history so don't blame the messenger. But you can skip this bit if you want (you scaredy-cats).

Chapter 21 - Colours

Friday 17th October 1519
Or the 13th day of the tonalpohualli *Aztec*
day-count calendar.

The sky was high and huge and impossibly blue, like
a sapphire on the horizon, shading to deep navy way
over towards the horizon. Towards the very edges
of outer space.

Beyond the city walls lay a lush carpet of green treetops.
Emerald green and dark greens, light asparagus and
avocado, olives and pistachios; lime and mint greens
stretching out to the boundaries of the empire.

And inside the city walls was a riot of colour; yellows,
oranges, browns and blues, and the temples and pyramids
were decorated with gold and jewels, all sparkling brightly
in the Mexican sunshine. Festival time was always an
excuse for a celebration.

But it was the Pyramid of the Sun that dominated the city.
Located at the end of the Avenue of the Dead, it was built
up around five massive stepped terraces and it towered
above the entire city of Teotihuacan. A temple was situated
at the uppermost level and below this, down through centre
of the pyramid ran a huge staircase, and today, the steps
were bathed in brilliant blood red.

From the top, bright crimsons flowed into scarlet, and
further down the pyramid darker ruby and mahogany
streams ebbed to the ground; a river of blood cascading
like a waterfall, as a tribute to their gods.

The Aztec people were religious and believed that their
gods were hungry. The people themselves were starving,
as their crops had once again failed. And so, to feed these
ravenous gods, they captured people from other tribes,

enslaved them and killed them as sacrifices.

Festivals and blood-drenched sacrifice was an almost continuous part of the Aztec ceremonial year. Each February, children were sacrificed to the maize gods on the mountain tops. In March, prisoners would fight to the death in gladiatorial contests, after which priests dressed up in their skins. In April, a maize goddess received her share of children. In June, there are sacrifices to the salt goddess. And so it went on, with an annual harvest of over 10,000 victims per year.

Two large stone tables sat before the temple, and four priests stood alongside, their costumes embroidered with fine gold and decorated with feathers. They were awaiting their next two human sacrifices, to join the hundreds already slaughtered that day. A huge audience had gathered in the plaza below, and they were singing and whistling expectantly.

Now would not be a good time for two strangers to drop in on the ceremony!

But the skies darkened, as a fine mist swirled around the temple at the top of the pyramid. Clouds swept in silently over the horizon and the brilliant blue sky turned into a gloomy slate grey blanket. Black clouds rolled in over the Avenue of the Dead like the angels of death.

And a small boy with fiery orange hair, along with an elderly man with a kilt and bushy moustache dropped out of the sky and landed on the sacrificial slabs.

Storm clouds rumbled like hot silver in the thunderous sky, and the senior priest, at first astonished, then with growing delight, approached the stone tables clutching a ceremonial knife made of flint, which had cut out two hundred hearts already that day. He had held the hearts aloft, still beating and squeezed the very lifeblood out of them, thinking each contained a fragment of the sun's heat, and therefore a dedication to the gods.

And these two newcomers, as unusual as they were, would make the most excellent sacrifices.

'Now would be a good time to squeeze out another little pump, George,' whispered Grandpa Jock, his eyes never leaving the high priest's blood-stained blade.

Chapter 22 - Home Alone 2

Present day

They all agreed that it would be best if they left
Mr Snuffles and Splat! at home, rather than take them
to the museum. Allison left a bowl of water in the kitchen,
and then rummaged around in Grandpa Jock's cupboards
until she found a tin of tuna, which she opened and tipped
into another bowl. The kittens seemed quite happy.

Little Pumpington Museum was a magnificent old
building, with high wide stairs and pillars at the front. It
opened at 10am every morning and closed at 5pm sharp.

Kenny, Allison and Wilberforce made their way there as
quickly as they could, with the parrot clinging onto
Kenny's shoulder again, not quite as firmly as before.

Once inside, they headed beyond the Natural History
section and ran passed all the exhibits of stuffed animals,
birds and reptiles. They passed by the Neanderthal
display, beyond the Animals of the Savannah and almost
stopped at Aztec Warrior exhibition. Until a bold
swashbuckler caught their attention!

In a glass cabinet, standing proudly in the centre of a
large pedestal marked The Caribbean Pirates was a
vicious buccaneer, hair-braided under a red bandana
and coins woven into his black beard. He held a silver
cutlass above his head and the small card at his feet
read 'Captain Jack Parrott'.

Allison shook her head. They'd met the real guy, Allison
had landed on top of him, and this display was just a
terrible rip-off from that Disney movie. But she guessed that
Little Pumpington Museum could never pay proper royalties
for the real thing, so they just made up their own displays.

But that's not why they had stopped. Allison, Kenny and

Wilberforce were now staring at his feet. Captain Jack Parrot, or the dummy dressed up badly to look like Captain Jack was standing on a small pile of golden coins.

Kenny looked around sharply. 'Stay here. I know where to go.'

With nobody looking, he ran around the side of the glass cabinet and disappeared through a small door at the back of the exhibits. Beyond this door was a set of steps down into the museum basement. The cellar was a treasure trove of mysterious artefacts, sealed boxes and wooden chests secured with chunky padlocks. Suits of armour were stacked alongside an Egyptian sarcophagus and a large moose head was propped on top of one particularly precarious pile of stuffed penguins. Kenny ran passed them all towards another door at the far end.

He opened it gingerly, crept inside and was now standing directly behind Captain Jack Parrott. He looked out beyond the glass, and signalled a cheeky little thumbs-up towards Allison and Wilberforce. Then he began picking up the gold coins and thrusting them into his pockets. Seconds later, he was back round the front of the display, looking very proud of himself.

Allison was standing by the display, whilst Wilberforce had hopped onto the barrier.

'I knew that door was there,' said Kenny proudly. 'I sneaked back there during a school trip a couple of years ago. My teacher went mental at the time.'

'You can't steal those coins,' hissed Allison.

'I'm only borrowing them,' replied Kenny. 'It was your idea to come here.'

'Yes but I wanted to see the coin collection,' Allison argued. 'To find out more about the coins in our treasure chest.'

'Technically, it's not really your treasure chest,' Wilberforce pointed out.

'Well, technically I've collected some coins,' nodded Kenny. 'Now what's the connection, smarty-pants?' Wilberforce sighed.

"I think he knows more than he's telling, Allison,' said Kenny, pointing towards the bird.

The parrot sighed again. 'Collections and connections,' he pondered. 'It is true, actually. All the gold in the world is or has been connected at one time or another… almost drawn together.' Kenny glanced at Allison, who raised both eyebrows. Wilberforce went on.

'Gold holds many more secrets, you know,' shrugged the bird. 'Traumatic moments of the past can be forged into the golden artefacts around them. And gold just doesn't absorb souls, it can absorb time. Gold can tell stories.'

Kenny pulled some of the coins from his pocket, and felt an energy and warmth in his hand. Was that his soul being slowly absorbed?

'That wooden chest…' declared Wilberforce, 'is a time-warp treasure trove!'

Go on, say it. You know you want to…

Chapter 23 - Geography

Friday 17th October 1519

'Well, that was a close call,' laughed Grandpa Jock, as he tucked into another bowl of spicy broth. 'Throw a few more beans into this, just to be sure.'

George rummaged around in his pocket and fetched out half a dozen of the yellow and green beans. The broth fizzed and crackled as soon as he threw them into the bowl and Grandpa Jock stirred them in with his wooden spoon.

'I really thought we were goners,' agreed George. 'That priest guy was going to chop us into mincemeat for sure.'

'Thank heavens for that rain, eh. As soon as it started, those chaps were on their knees, bowing and worshiping us,' smiled Grandpa Jock, standing. 'And it's still pouring down outside.'

They were sitting inside the temple at the top of the Pyramid of the Sun. Grandpa Jock walked towards the doorway and watched the torrents of water hammering down on the steps, washing away the blood stains. Forks of lightning occasionally pierced the skies, which were still black with storm clouds, and thunder clapped like giant hands applauding.

'Thunderbolts and lightning, very, very frightening indeed,' giggled Grandpa Jock. 'Galileo.'

'What?' gasped George, and as he turned, his nostrils were filled with a sickeningly sweet, metallic stench wafting up from the steps. The acidic rawness caught the back of his throat with a vile pungency and he gagged.

'Urrgh. It doesn't half stink about here,' groaned George. 'It's worse than your bum, Grandpa.'

'History does smell, doesn't it?' agreed Grandpa Jock.

'That bakery in Pudding Lane was stinking of stale sweat, and those pirates hadn't washed in weeks.'

'But where are we, and when are we, Grandpa?'

'If I know my geography, my best guess is that we're in the middle of Mexico somewhere, probably hundreds of years in the past, judging by their clothes and the city itself. I reckon these guys are Aztecs,' Grandpa Jock went on.

'And these lads must've been killing their slaves all day,' nodded Grandpa Jock, staring down the Avenue of the Dead towards the Pyramid of the Moon. 'They must've been pretty desperate to appease their gods. I think they just needed the rains to come.'

George started to scratch his face and chest again, even though his rash was improving, and Grandpa Jock had warned him not scratch, like, a million times. He turned, as one of the priests entered from a doorway at the back of the temple.

The priest's eyes were red and swollen, and he walked slowly, as if every bone in his body ached. He was struggling to carry another tray, not broth this time, but delicate nibbles drizzled with honey. The poor priest set the tray down and shambled away.

Grandpa Jock stepped forward, picked up one of the treats and crunched into it. 'These are lovely,' he said, munching into another one. 'I wonder what they are?'

'Er, Grandpa, we studied the Aztecs in school.' George paused. 'I think those might be grasshoppers, or crickets.'

Grandpa Jock stopped chewing, as a look of disgust crossed his face. He screwed up his mouth, picked little bits of grasshopper leg out of his teeth, and spat a ball of sticky insect goo across the room. The honey glob stuck fast to the wall.

'Grasshoppers!' yelled the old geezer, his face turning sickly pale.

'You ate stick insects once before, Grandpa. Remember?' laughed George.

'That's because I thought they were Twiglets,' moaned Grandpa Jock. 'Not real insects. I'm not even a celebrity.'

'Well, the priests believe that we brought the rains,' shrugged George. 'The way they were worshipping us. And despite their famine, they were happy to feed us.'

Grandpa Jock stopped and stared at the bowls lying on the trays. 'So, what do you think was in that broth then?'

George chuckled. 'Definitely beans, and maybe chicken.' Grandpa Jock let out a sigh of relief. 'Or lizards, frogs or salamanders.' Grandpa Jock began to turn pale again.

'And the Aztec's put chilli in almost everything,' George sniggered. 'But I love this chocolate drink they gave us. It must be made out of cocoa beans.'

'More beans,' groaned Grandpa Jock. 'That's what got us into this mess to begin with.'

Just then, the clouds began to part and golden yellow sunshine lit up the pyramid. George and his grandfather walked across to the temple entrance as a brilliant double rainbow shone down on the city of Teotihuacan.

'I wonder where that rainbow ends?' wondered Grandpa Jock, as he stared across the rooftops and the smaller pyramids and the Avenue of the Dead.

'You're old, Grandpa, were rainbows black and white when you were a boy?' laughed George.

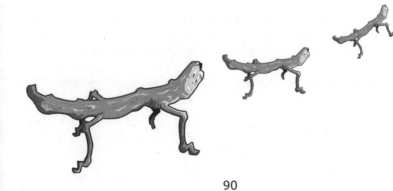

Chapter 24 - Rainbows

Leprechaun time

'Follow the rainbows,
Go through that door.
I beez feeding my greed,
And I beez wanting more.'

The leprechaun's eyes sparkled as he watched George and Grandpa Jock take the main steps down from the temple at the top of the Pyramid of the Sun. The storm clouds were clearing, and to the east, the sky was a crystal blue palette of dripping colour. Double rainbows arched across from the forest, over the city to the Pyramid of the Moon at the end of the avenue, like a promise.

'It beez coming together now, cauldron,' whispered Tiny Tom, as he danced around in the darkness. 'Not long, not long.'

And then the little man stopped skipping, turned back to the pool and clasped his hands together. His furtive eyes darted from side to side, the mental cogs inside his head stretching one step, then two steps beyond. The next part of his plan was hatching, as he swirled the waters with his finger, time ebbing and flowing, forwards and backwards and deeper.

'Gold, gold, and the absence of light,' sighed the leprechaun.

'Turn black now, what once was white.'

A woman's face shimmered into view in the larger pool. There was hustle and bustle behind her and the wooden buildings were tightly packed in never-ending rows. Her clothes were once smart but now older, and she wore a shawl wrapped around her shoulders.

'Mincewind, Mincewind, show them the way.' Tiny Tom hissed as he spoke. 'Lead them to poison, death and decay.'

And as he stirred the larger pool a glimmer of light rippled across the smaller one. A prism of light shimmered, all the colours of the world spreading out across the cave, as the clouds cleared. The leprechaun turned to look into the puddle, and whispered…

'Beanz, beanz, the musical fruit.

Blast away and bring me my loot.

Gold, gold, no good for your heart.

If you drop all that you're going back to the start.'

Tiny Tom's fingers danced on his golden teeth, as his evil little eyes darted back and forth. His greed was like a bottomless pit which had exhausted the leprechaun throughout his life, in an endless effort to satisfy that need without ever reaching satisfaction.

Chapter 25 - Aztecs

Friday 17th October 1519

After two centuries of warfare and migration, the Aztecs had settled in the Valley of Mexico. They'd built houses and homes and cities. They were well-organised and incredibly successful. They had engineers, traders and farmers.

A system of free education was set up. Every child went to school; boys, girls, and even their slaves. Children were taught to honour proper behaviour and learn a specialised skill. Teachers were highly respected professionals.

The Aztecs were also talented craftsmen, learning to use gold, silver, paints and clay in their art and jewellery. Much of the Aztec art was colourful and religious, and as George and Grandpa Jock walked through the marketplace, they saw stalls filled with silver rings and brooches made from jade, along with decorated clay pots. Food stalls were selling beans, quesadillas, frogs and lizards. But nobody was buying anything… and nobody was selling anything.

People were just sitting around, covering their eyes from the sun. Children were lying listless beneath the stalls in the shade. Rich noblemen and women wore colourful clothes embroidered with features, and carried fans made of feathers but many of them were red-faced and sweating, flapping their fans furiously.

'Feathers are a sign of status here, Grandpa,' whispered George. 'If you are a commoner, and you're caught carrying a feather, you'll be put to death.'

'They teach ye some yucky things in school nowadays, lad,' grunted Grandpa Jock. 'But I guess they needed to find all those people to sacrifice from somewhere.'

'The Aztecs killed the men they captured in battle,' said George quietly, 'but also the women and children too. Their laws were very harsh.'

'And they called this *civilisation?*'

'One of the biggest civilisations in the world, Grandpa, back in the day,' replied George. 'And my teacher says that we need to learn from history, so we don't repeat ourselves.'

'What the… ?' gasped Grandpa Jock.

"I said, we need to learn from history, so we don't repeat ourselves.' echoed George.

'No, lad. Look.' Grandpa Jock was pointing towards the end of the rainbows, now almost touching the cloth hanging outside the Pyramid of the Moon. The cloth banner stretched over the entrance to the temple and read 'Farmers' Market'. George gulped but even though there was nobody standing there; no little green men, no guards and no priests. The doors leading inside the pyramid were wide open and a golden light shone out from within.

'How's your bottom doing, Grandpa,' whispered George. 'I have the feeling we might need a quick getaway.'

'Don't you worry about that, lad. My belly has been brewing away for some time now,' and the old Scotsman winked.

They walked closer, and just inside the huge limestone doors, slumped against the walls, were two Aztec guards. Their spears had fallen to the floor too and both men were covered with a red rash. Their arms, their chests, their faces, even their legs.

'Keep going,' urged Grandpa Jock. 'Don't look!' and they ran past the guards, towards the golden glow. Beyond the doors lay a massive chamber filled with stone statues, idols, jewels, jade, feathers and much, much more.

In the corner lay a small bag, overflowing with golden discs, shining brightly, as if the light came from within.

'There you are again, George,' laughed Grandpa Jock, as he picked up one of the coins. He paused, thinking aloud. 'My coin, your bag of gold, the pirate's treasure chest, now these ones. Life throws us challenges and every challenge comes with rainbows and lights to conquer it. I think the secret is in the gold, lad.'

'I agree with you, Grandpa,' blurted George. 'But it's time to get out of here.'

George grabbed the bag and turned. He was now staring at a large group of priests and warriors, every one of them was holding a spear, or clubs or swords or flint daggers or any other manner of painful-looking items. Their bodies were splattered with blood and their faces painted with lines and dots, black soot around their eyes and blue shade beneath on their cheeks. Their lips and ears were pierced with bone, and the warriors at the front were dressed as eagles and jaguars. Nobody looked friendly.

They stepped forward menacingly. The first warrior lifted his club, a vicious length of hardwood embedded with flint, excellent for skull crushing and he gave out a scream of anger and rage and... cough, and mucus, and splutter, and he fell down onto the earthen floor.

Behind him, other warriors and priests were choking and sneezing. Their heavy, red eyelids were watering, and as they fell to their knees, they began scratching and clawing at the red blotchy patches that were spreading across their bodies.

'What's wrong with them,' George asked nervously.

'I don't know,' replied Grandpa Jock. 'But whatever it is, it won't be good for us. They were sacrificing people when they thought their gods were angry... angry enough to hold back the rains. Who do you think will be killed next if their gods sent them a plague?'

'A plague? Who's sent them a plague?' quivered George.

'I'm not one to point the finger George, but maybe you did,' shouted Grandpa Jock. 'I think you've given them the measles.'

Chapter 26 - Blame Game

Personally, little readers, I think that was a bit harsh on George. The poor lad had been feeling under the weather for a few days and how was he to know that he was still infectious.

It's just like when I visit schools as an author. Suddenly I am surrounded by hundreds of grotty little kids, coughing and spluttering and picking their noses. And don't pretend to be shocked, little reader, just look around you. Little kids can be disgusting... and riddled with diseases.

That's why I carry antiseptic throat spray with me, and bacterial hand-gel and cough sweets. And I am surprised that I haven't caught lice yet!

But anyway, the Aztecs empire would crumble after 1519 when the Spanish conquistador, Hernan Cortes, arrived. The Aztecs thought he was a gift from their gods and he was welcomed with open arms.

Except he was infected with European diseases such as measles, smallpox, mumps, influenza and typhoid. And those poor, blood-thirsty, human-sacrificing Aztecs were wiped out in these epidemics in the years that followed. They had no defence against the infections and more than 20 millions people died.

In a few short years, the culture and structure of one of the greatest empires in history virtually vanished. The Aztec Empire collapsed.

But don't blame George!

Chapter 27 - Me too!

Present day

'You go first.'

'No, you go first.'

'You eat it.'

'No, you eat it.'

'You first.'

'No, you go first.'

'Make the parrot go first!'

'I really do not think it would be appropriate to force feed curry into the beak of an unwilling bird,' said Wilberforce, fluffing up his feathers again.

Allison, Kenny and Wilberforce had returned from the museum and were now back in Grandpa Jock's kitchen. The pot of time-travelling tandoori was still sitting on the hob, and was now thicker and gloopier than ever. The colour could be described as brown, it might've been green and underneath the layer of crust that was forming on the top, it definitely looked stale yellow. Allison poked at the mush with a spoon.

'You were willing to try it with George earlier,' said Allison, stopping to think if that was earlier today, or yesterday, or even the day before that. Time had merged into a multi-layer mishmash of memories.

'Yes but that was just bravado,' argued Kenny. 'It was a

guy-thing. We were just egging each other on.'

'You boys are so stupid,' replied Allison, shaking her head. 'Always trying to look brave and cool in front of your mates. Why can't you just admit stuff?'

'Admit what?' answered Kenny, unsure where the conversation was going, and beginning to feel nervous.

'Oh I don't know. Admit the kittens are cute for example,' said Allison, pointing over at the box in the corner. It was filled with two fluffy balls of ginger fur. 'Cute is still cute. Kittens are adorable and boys can't admit it. You think it's unmanly.'

'It's not my fault that stupid society says boys have to act tough all the time,' Kenny argued.

'No you don't,' replied Allison. 'Just be yourself.'

'Modern society does create stereotypes that pressure boys to act in certain ways,' brooded Wilberforce. 'Boys do not always have to wear blue, just as girls do not always need to wear pink. In fact, pink was considered a boy's colour until after World War Two. Before that, military uniforms were red, so boys were expected to wear pink. Blue was thought to be more delicate and dainty, and therefore, a girl's colour.'

'Quick, stop him,' smiled Allison. 'He's gone off on one again.'

'For centuries before that, all children wore white dresses for practical purposes,' continued Wilberforce. 'Easily lifted to change a baby's nappy, and then easily bleached when said nappy inevitably exploded.'

'Say something, Kenny. This is disgusting.'

'Okay, okay,' shrugged Kenny. 'I suppose the kittens are kinda cute. There, I said it. Happy?'

'And say that you are too scared to eat that curry,' giggled Allison.

'I'm not too scared.' Kenny knew he was being gently

pushed into a corner. 'It's just that I'm… erm…
not that hungry.'

'It's only one spoonful,' laughed Allison, and then she
stopped herself. Girls can be tough too, she thought. And
in one swift movement, she pushed Kenny back with her
left hand and scooped up a spoonful of curry with her right.
Wilberforce flapped backwards and hovered in the air.
Allison thrust the spoon into her mouth and swallowed
the curry. And another spoonful. And another, until the
pot was empty.

'Well,' asked Kenny, rather reluctantly. He glanced down
at Allison's tummy. 'Is it kicking in yet?'

'Of course it is not *kicking in*, as you so delicately put it,
Kenneth,' declared Wilberforce, settling down on the back
of a kitchen chair. 'I am sure it takes longer than…'

A thunderous, rasping juggernaut of a fart launched itself
from Allison's behind, so fast and furious that the poor girl
had no idea what hit her.

'Or perhaps the beans have been maturing,' coughed
the parrot, backtracking wildly, and jumping onto
Allison's shoulder.

'See, girls pump too,' gasped Allison, doubling over a
chair, gas clouds transforming the kitchen into a hazy,
green wobble. Kenny grabbed Allison's hand.

Chapter 28 - To beez or not to beez

Monday 26th August 1602

'POOOOOOOooooooooo0000000000whaaarrrrrrrrr!!!!'

'That stinks, Grandpa. That really, really stinks,' groaned George, waving his hand back and forth across his face. In the other hand, he held tightly onto his bag of gold coins.

'Sorry about that lad but I was just glad to be getting out of that pyramid,' agreed Grandpa Jock, scratching his bottom. There was still a small trail of smoke drifting out from underneath his kilt.

'I mean, even stink would say that stinks! Grandpa,' George went on. 'You've got to give us a warning before dropping another one of those whoppers.'

George was still coughing and wafting his arms around but the smell was not getting any better. If anything, the smell was getting worse. Grandpa Jock poked his head out of the little wooden shack they were standing in, and looked around.

The street was small, too small to deserve to be called a street, really. It was narrow, and the wooden buildings towered high above their heads. They were tightly packed together and there was a sign at the end that read 'Tanners Row'.

''Ere, wot you standing 'round there for?' screeched a voice from behind them.

Grandpa Jock and George both turned quickly, and a sharply-angled face thrust itself into George's view. The woman might've been about thirty years old, or forty, or even fifty; George couldn't be sure. She had kind, sparkling eyes and a long thin face.

Her cheeks was slathered with white grease, and close up

George could see her face was covered in dozens of tiny scars. And closer up, she was stinking. It was a spoiled, rancid pong like stale chips from an old deep-fat fryer.

''Aven't I seen you somewhere before?' said the woman, who was staring at George and examining every inch of his face. Then she smiled, and her whole mouth turned black. Her teeth were rotten, with one or two beginning to drop out.

'Ha, I see you noticing my sweet tooth,' the woman laughed. 'Thank you. I spends a fortune on sugar these days but black is the new white, as they say.'

'We've been devouring that stuff since old Raleigh brought it back from the Caribbean recently. Even good Queen Bess' teeth have turned black,' she smiled. 'It's all the fashion now. Honey without bees.'

'White gold,' she went on. 'More expensive anyhow but my customers in the tea-room can't get enough of it,' and she waved her hand across a large blackboard menu on the wall.

Steamed swan in sugar sauce, it read with *Baked rabbit with sugared oysters* written beneath it. Next to it sat another board that read '*The Tragical Historie of Hamlet at the Globe Theatre - Tickets now on Sale.*'

The woman walked back into her tea-room,wrapping her tattered shawl around her shoulders, and beckoned the two lads to follow her. 'You can call me Mrs Mincewind,' said Mrs Mincewind. 'And I heard you coughing, young man, so perhaps you would like something to drink?'

'Just water, please,' asked George, still no idea where or when he was.

'Water?' screeched Mrs Mincewind. 'You can't drink water. You should have beer. That's much better for you.'

'Just take the beer, lad,' whispered Grandpa Jock. 'It'll be fine.'

And George picked up the large tankard which Mrs Mincewind had placed on the counter. It was frothy and tasted like very weak malt. George finished the drink quickly and pushed the tankard back. 'Thank you,' he said quietly.

'I brews me own,' she announced proudly. 'Much safer than that mucky old water nonsense.' And the woman took the tankard back over to the sink.

George whispered, 'Why is her face painted, Grandpa? She looks like a clown.'

'I think it's a kind of grease made from pig lard, lad,' replied Grandpa Jock, out of the corner of his mouth. 'To cover her smallpox scars. Either that or an old make-up made from lead but that would be poisonous.'

'Smallpox,' gasped George. 'Is she contagious?'

'Don't think so,' replied Grandpa Jock. 'People are only contagious if they have a rash, so watch out.'

'What a marvellous establishment you have here, Mrs Mincewind,' proclaimed Grandpa Jock, changing the subject in his poshest voice. George turned to stare at him.

'Why thank you, sir,' bowed Mrs Mincewind, also now talking in her poshest accent. 'It's not often we serve such a fine gentleman wearing a kilt.' Grandpa Jock twiddled the corner of his moustache.

'Especially when Mr Mincewind has been away fighting with the Dutch these last two winters.' George thought that Mrs Mincewind winked at his grandfather but decided it was just her large, elaborate eyelashes sticking together.

'And what an unusual aroma you have created throughout your tea-rooms.' Grandpa Jock was waltzing between the tables across the room.

'Thank you again, sir,' twittered Mrs Mincewind, her eyelashes fluttering once more. 'We were so tired of people throwing their, ahem, waste out into the street that we decided to build our privy over the sewers. Runs straight into the River Thames… much fresher that way.'

'Oh how marvellous,' enthused Grandpa Jock, clapping his hands together.

'Of course, they do become blocked occasionally, with a build-up of dead animals and other unpleasant… erm, what-nots,' simpered Mrs Mincewind, 'but that's the price you have to pay for good hygiene these days.'

'Of course,' agreed Grandpa Jock. 'And perhaps you can help us, my dear. We are looking for…'

'I know exactly what you're looking for!' Mrs Mincewind's eyelashes stuck together again.

'You beez wanting Mr Shakespeare then. Go to the Globe!' growled a voice with an Irish accent deep within Mrs Mincewind's throat. She jumped back, startled, unsure herself where this demonic voice had come from. George and Grandpa Jock looked at each other and gulped.

'Well, er… you really must excuse us, madam,' stuttered Grandpa Jock, wiping his hands on his kilt and striding towards the door. 'We have an appointment with er… somebody.'

'When will you be wanting your rabbit and oysters?' called Mrs Mincewind but it was too late. Grandpa Jock had dragged George by the scruff of the neck out the front door and into the street.

'Touch nothing, George. This place is rife.'

'What did you mean, Grandpa?'

'They build their toilets over open sewers,' barfed Grandpa Jock. 'They overflow, they flood the streets with sh… sh… shtuff.'

'But where are we?'

'London, lad. It must be about the early 1600's because that play Hamlet has started and Queen Elizabeth the First is still alive,' Grandpa Jock went on.

'And the smell wasn't just the sewers. It's called Tanners

Row because of all the tanneries, where they make leather.'
Grandpa Jock was walking and talking briskly, trying to get
away from the stench. 'They make leather, by soaking the
cow hides in poo and wee.'

George put his hand over his mouth and Grandpa Jock
kept pulling his arm, away from Tanners Row. The stink was
almost overpowering now.

'Glue and soap was also made in a tannery, from animal
fat and bones.' Grandpa Jock was almost running now.
'And what you're smelling is the stale stench of nearly half a
million people living together, and washing, or not washing
together. Queen Elizabeth was known to say that she 'had a
bath once a month, whether she needed to or not.'

George yakked at the back of this throat.

They ran past row after row of narrow wooden houses,
each one rickety and ready to fall down. And as they ran
past a courtyard, George spied a large black-furred bear
chained up. It was a giant creature, and possibly the
saddest animal George had ever seen. The bear sat in the
corner of the garden, wounded and bleeding, its thick iron
chain cutting into one of its legs.

'Yeah, bear-baiting. They called that a sport, back in the
day,' groaned Grandpa Jock sadly, pulling George onwards.
'Some people chose to look the other way but they could
never say they did not know about stuff like that.'

'I wish we could do something to help, Grandpa.'

'Time will change everything if you wait long enough, lad,'
Grandpa Jock added, 'And as long as people with good
heads and good hearts have the courage. Right now, we
have our own problems.'

Chapter 29 - Ancient Egypt

The sixth day of Ahket III in the month of Osiris and 39th year of Ptolemy
Or Sunday 6th April, 51BC

If anyone was paying attention to the edge of the River Nile that day, they might've seen a small man, dressed in a green suit with a floppy hat and pointed little boots. He was crawling around in the reeds at the edge of the water, muttering to himself.

And if anyone was watching closely, they might just have seen that the little man had appeared, as if from nowhere, flopping into the water. Not there one minute, there the next.

But, of course, nobody was paying attention to the water that day. Not that there was much water, just muddy puddles and dried, cracked soil towards the river banks. No rain had fallen on Egypt for over a year.

However, there was something far more spectacular taking place up by the temple in front of a magnificent pyramid. A huge crowd had gathered and a ferocious man wearing sandals, a loin cloth and decorated headdress was holding a high priest's golden staff. In his other hand was a large, brown snake; its body round and stout, with a long tail.

At his feet knelt a young woman. She was no more than 18 years old, with a prominent nose, sharply pointed chin and thin lips. Her forehead sloped backwards and her eyes were dark and striking. She held her head up proudly, as if daring the priest.

With a high-pitched shriek, the man with the golden staff cried out.

'No longer shall we ruled by a woman. Egypt deserves a king!' he shouted. 'Death to Cleopatra!'

The high priest squeezed the snake tightly around its neck, and its tongue flicked in and out, tasting the warm air. The priest squeezed the reptile again, baring a pair of vicious fangs and held the writhing creature closer to her throat.

Nobody was watching the water edge. Nobody was listening to the water edge.

Because if anyone had been listening to the little man in the river, they might just have heard him whisper…

'Water, water, everywhere.
My pool can takez me anywhere,
From seas to clouds, to rains then lakes
Slithers through time, like curious snakes.'

Chapter 30 - Something Wicked This Way Comes

Monday 26th August 1602

They ran on and on, through the streets of London, jumping over rivers of poo and puddles of pee. Brown sludge was everywhere and occasionally George would see small children with bare feet dancing and playing in the mud.

'Watch the poo there,' shouted Grandpa Jock, pulling George's arm. 'And there.'

'Touch nothing,' he went on. 'Don't drink the water, it's filthy. Beer is safer because it's been boiled, and it's very weak. Even children drank beer right up to the Victorian days. Mrs Mincewind said she brewed her own.'

'Okay Grandpa,' agreed George. 'I don't want to catch anything.'

'And what was up with her voice at the end,' said Grandpa Jock, as they slowed down. 'She sounded evil, like she'd been possessed by a demon.'

'I've heard that voice before, Grandpa.' George paused, pulling at his bottom lip and thinking hard.

'You're right, lad,' nodded Grandpa Jock, 'I remember hearing that voice on the pirate ship too.'

'No, I mean before that.' George stopped. Perhaps Mrs Mincewind was possessed by mean spirits or at least, one mean spirit in particular…

'And that accent,' gasped Grandpa Jock. 'It definitely sounded Irish, so…' He stopped in mid-sentence, his little brain ticking over and over, all the clues and the cogs and the gears were finally coming together.

'I know where I heard that voice,' George spluttered. 'That was Tiny Tom, at the farmers' market. The little guy who gave me those beans. He's behind all this!'

'Think about it, lad. Pots of gold and rainbows and magic

beans, and all that mad stuff,' shouted Grandpa Jock. 'He's a leprechaun!'

'A leprechaun?' repeated George.

'Sure he is, the little fellow tricked you into taking his magic beans,' continued the old Scotsman. 'He didn't want that old cow suit. He wanted us to find his gold for him! Leprechauns trick people with their get-rich-quick schemes, and their pots of gold hidden at the end of a rainbow. We are messing with things beyond our understanding, lad.'

'Mrs Mincewind, or the leprechaun said we should seek out Mr Shakespeare,' added George. 'She said we should go to the Globe.'

'Aye, lad. She meant the Globe Theatre. I think we're heading in the right direction.'

'I think she fancied you, Grandpa.' George sniggered as he said this.

'And I can think of nothing worse,' Grandpa Jock winked, 'than kissing someone whose face is covered in rotten pig grease. I was only using my charms to find our next clue. And by the pricking of my thumbs, something wicked this way comes.'

Grandpa Jock gave George the thumbs-up and winked again as they turned the corner… and bumped into a tall, slim man, rather handsome with a small mouth and long hair combed back, revealing his balding forehead. He had a thin wispy beard and a curled moustache.

The man wore a padded, laced doublet of a rich burgundy red, and in his hand he carried a small velvet purse. It jingled as he came to a complete halt.

'Come, come, thou frothy hedge-born apple-johns, watch where thou steps,' the man blurted out, taking a pace back. He looked down at George and caught sight of Grandpa Jock's kilt.

'Aah, a Scotsman,' said the man, a smile spreading

across his face. 'Once a scurvy companion but in thy face I see the map of honour, truth and loyalty. Methinks I should enjoy writing a Scottish play one day.'

Grandpa Jock, for once lost for words, turned to George and shook his head.

'Sorry, sir,' George stammered. 'We were in a bit of a hurry. We were looking for the Globe Theatre.'

'The Globe indeed, young sir,' declared the man. 'Where all the world's a stage, And all the men and women merely players. You have such fine taste for one so young.'

'Mrs Mincewind said we should go there... to look for Mr Shakespeare.'

'Urgh, Mincewind,' groaned the gentleman. 'That lump of foul deformity, the rankest compound of villainous smell that ever offended nostril. More of her conversation would infect my brain.'

'I think we've found Mr Shakespeare, George,' quivered Grandpa Jock, pointing. 'That's him.'

George turned. 'You're him? You are William Shakespeare? The playwright?'

'The very same, young sir. William Shakespeare at your service.' And the man bowed low and graciously. 'And how may I help you?'

'W-w-well,' George stuttered, 'I'm not really sure. We've been following a trail, sort of, through time, I think. You see, we're from the future and...' George paused, not sure if he was making any sense but Shakespeare just looked down upon the boy and smiled.

"To-morrow, and to-morrow, and to-morrow,' he whispered. 'Creeps on from day to day. To the last syllable of recorded time. And all our yesterdays light the way.'

'Sorry, what's that meant to mean?' asked Grandpa Jock, butting in and scratching his head.

'I am not entirely sure,' replied William Shakespeare. 'The

boy was talking about time…
and the words just popped
into my head. I rather like
them.'

'Listen, bard. We're looking
for some coins and it's the
only way we're going to get
back home and stop that
leprechaun.' Grandpa Jock
was clenching his false teeth
tightly again.

'Ah yes, leprechauns…
mischievous and troublesome
little tricksters, like gnomes and
fairies,' nodded Shakespeare, eyeing them carefully. 'And
coins, you say. What kind of coins?'

'Like these ones.' George shook the bag in his hand.

'Or these ones,' replied Shakespeare, shaking the purse
in his hand.

'Careful, George,' snapped Grandpa Jock, looking around
at the narrow streets. 'You don't want to be showing your
gold around these parts.'

The playwright opened the drawstring on his velvet bag,
reached in and pulled out a gold coin. The coin sparkled,
despite the dull, grey afternoon. George recognised it
immediately.

'Careful, Willy,' hissed Grandpa Jock again.

'Tish and tosh, sir. These baubles are a child's mere
plaything… nothing but fool's gold,' laughed William
Shakespeare. 'See here, there is a boy's head on one side
and strange animal on the other.'

'Where did you get them from?' George asked, trying not
to raise any suspicions.

'That was the strangest thing,' Shakespeare replied.

'I was in my lodgings writing my next play, a tragedy entitled Antony and Cleopatra, set in Egypt you know, when I heard a-clattering down the chimney. And there I found these coins.'

'And do you recognise the boy's face?' smirked Grandpa Jock.

Shakespeare stopped and stared at the coin again. He flipped it around in his fingers and looked from George to the coin, and back again.

'Ye gods, sir! It is you!' jabbered the bard. 'What in devil's name were you doing on my rooftop?'

George opened up his bag and removed a few coins. He held them in the palm of his hand, and turned them over to show off his head on each one. Shakespeare lay his coin next to George's and compared them.

'I am so sorry, Mr Shakespeare sir, erm...' George paused, thinking furiously. 'But... erm... a naughty magpie snatched up one of my bags of coins,' George lied. 'And flew off with them. The bird must've dropped them down your chimney.'

'Well, I can see the resemblance of course,' muttered Shakespeare. 'But what does a boy want with fool's gold?'

'Er... I play with my treasure, sir, when I pretend to be Walter Raleigh returning from El Dorado, the lost city of gold,' smiled George sweetly. Grandpa Jock's eyes widened; shocked, surprised and not a little bit impressed by the quality of his grandson's tall tale.

'Well, I suppose fair is foul and foul is fair,' sighed the bard. 'When magpies hover through this filthy air.' And he handed the purse over to George. 'I am sure I will find some other trinkets to rehearse with.'

'Thank you, Sir William,' bowed George.

'Alas, boy, do not call me 'Sir'. I am not, nor ever will be, a knight of the realm.' Shakespeare waved his hand away.

'That is the preserve of government officials, the military and other such noblemen. I am but a lowly author.'

'We better get going, George. We've kept Mr Shakespeare back long enough,' said Grandpa Jock as he pulled at George's sleeve and put his hand up to his forehead four or five times in quick salutes. 'And thank you again. Meeting William Shakespeare is a brilliant story to tell people.'

'Your life is just a tale, told by an idiot,' laughed the bard. 'Full of sound and fury.'

As soon as they were round the corner, Grandpa Jock stopped and turned back, slightly slow in the uptake. 'Who's he calling an idiot? I've got a good mind to give him a ruddy good punch up the bottom.'

'You shouldn't go around hitting people, Grandpa,' said George. 'And anyway, he gave us the gold we were looking for, no problems.'

'Aye lad, and if I catch you telling great big porky-pies like that again, you'll be the one in trouble,' laughed Grandpa Jock. 'Naughty magpies, my bum!"

'And talking about bums, Grandpa, are you feeling any bottom build-ups again.'

'Glad you asked, lad. Because I've been holding back a blast for ages.'

Chapter 31 - Cave

Leprechaun time

As the smoke cleared, and the girl, the boy and the parrot stopped coughing, they all opened their eyes.

'It is somewhat dark in here, is it not,' stated a voice with a feathery lilt.

'I can't see a thing,' replied the boy.

'I think I've gone blind.'

Allison blinked, and blinked again. She stretched her eyes as wide as they could go… they were definitely open… or at least she thought her eyes were open. She felt her eyelids move again. Darkness lay in front of her. It was a velvet black, starless darkness, a vast hole in space and time.

But there was light behind them, she could sense it, see it dancing on her fingers, feel it streaming past, outlining the darkness ahead… into an ebony black cavern.

And there was a faint trickle of water behind them too.

Chapter 32 - Ancient Aliens

*The sixth day of Ahket III in the month of Osiris and 39th
year of Ptolemy
Or Sunday 6th April, 51BC*

As thunderous clouds broke wind above,

And soon the storm clouds parted.

An old man may take pleasant relief,

As man and boy both ~~farted~~ departed.

And arrived in a lush, green courtyard. The air was warm
and humid, yet the gardens were alive with flowers and
plants of every kind. Servants carrying pots of water ran
trembling into the corridors beyond, believing that Gods
had appeared from the skies.

'Where are we this time, Grandpa?' asked George,
walking towards the large arched doorway at the end of the
garden. The bright sunshine was spread across most of the
courtyard but this corner was darker and cooler, and the
walls were covered with ornate carvings.

Grandpa Jock touched the walls and stroked the
hieroglyphs. 'I'm not sure, lad,' he replied. 'But a wild guess
would say Egypt.'

'You are only saying that because this place stinks of
camel dung,' laughed George and he walked across
the painted figures on the walls. He scratched his
head, puzzling over the artwork, whilst Grandpa Jock
scratched his bottom, puzzling over the painful stinging
in his rear end.

'That was our biggest blast yet,' he groaned. 'The sorest one too. I reckon it's taken us further back in time than ever. Might be two or even three thousand years ago.'

The corridor into which they now walked was like a museum, with large statues of dog-headed Gods and bird-heads Gods and cats stretching out regally on golden plinths. The walls were decorated with more pictures and carvings, and at the far end appeared to be a golden throne room, shining brightly, casting golden shadows out like ripples.

'Look at this one, Grandpa.' George was crouched down by the wall. The carvings depicted lots of shapes in different styles and images. There were temples and pillars, fish, sea creatures and people, and hovering above them all was a little helicopter at the top.

'Is that.. a helicopter, Grandpa?'

'Can't be, lad. These were craved thousands of years before you were born... before helicopters were invented.'

'And look at this one, Grandpa,' squealed George, pointing at a large saucer-shaped craft surrounded by small Egyptians and birds and strange symbols. The object was larger than the other carvings, and seemed to fly above them all. It had three legs and three ports holes around its centre.

George and Grandpa Jock stared in amazement.

'Not more aliens,' groaned Grandpa Jock.

'What do you mean 'more aliens', Grandpa? We haven't met any aliens.' George had narrowed his eyes and was looking intently into his grandfather's face.

'We've seen pirates and pyramids. We met William Shakespeare, and one or both of us may have started the Great Fire of London,' declared George. 'But we have not met any aliens.'

'Pyramids?' puzzled Grandpa Jock, pulling at his moustache again. 'Pyramids, George! They were built almost the same, all around the world… we saw one in Mexico but they can be found in Africa, Indian, Peru and China, as well as Egypt.'

'They were built using millions of massive stone blocks that weighted up to two tons each.' Grandpa Jock was in full flow, as his little Scottish legs danced on the sand floor. 'They were amazing feats of engineering, and of course, the ancient peoples had no technology or modern construction equipment to help them.'

'So?'

'So some people think that the pyramids all around the world were built by aliens! As power plants or energy portals and landing platforms for alien spacecraft.'

'No chance,' argued George, thinking that perhaps his grandfather had finally lost his marbles.

'What's that then?' said Grandpa Jock, pointing towards the as-yet-unidentfied flying object.

'I don't believe it,' George said, turning his back.

'You are too young to realise that certain things are impossible, George, so you should do them anyway,' marvelled Grandpa Jock. 'Two days ago you thought time-travel was impossible but here you are.'

George paused and thought back on everything he had witnessed, the wonders he had seen and the journey, however unlikely, he had been on. He had never questioned it, well, perhaps only slightly, but still he believed enough to go on.

'To believe a thing impossible is to make it so,' whispered Grandpa Jock. 'Never stop believing, lad. It always seems impossible until it's done. At least, that's what Wilberforce said.'

They walked on towards the shimmering light and the throne room opened up into a huge gallery. More enormous statues lined the walls, designed to make the visitors feel small and unworthy, and at the far end stood a huge stone chair. Sitting on the top of the throne was a blue and yellow bird, and curled around the legs of the chair were two ginger cats.

The cats turned their heads slowly when Grandpa Jock and George stepped in the gallery but they saw nothing interesting and closed their eyes again. They lay there, regally and lazily, enjoying the comfort of their gilt cushions placed at the bottom of the throne.

'Hey, it's that parrot again,' shouted George.

'Well, technically I am a blue Macaw, young man,' replied the parrot with distaste. 'Rare, prized and, in this case, singularly unique.' The bird fluffed up its feathers again, and once smooth, held its head aloft. George and Grandpa Jock continued to stare at the bird, their constant glare rather unsettling.

The parrot glanced at them for a second, then turned away. He glanced again, pretending not to notice before finally huffing and turning towards the two lads.

'Can I help you?' snapped the bird with some annoyance.

'Have I seen you somewhere before?' asked Grandpa Jock, creeping closer. The bird peered down his beak towards them.

'Have we met?' quizzed the parrot. 'I think not. Have we met before? I am certain not.'

'But your name is Wilberforce, isn't it?' replied Grandpa Jock.

'Or are we still to meet?' smirked the bird. 'One day, in the future perhaps. And by the look on your face, old man, we may have met already. Do you believe that time flies? Or bends? Or warps?' If a beak could bend, then the parrot would be grinning from ear to ear.

'How old are you?' asked Grandpa Jock.

'Now, or then,' replied the bird. 'Or perhaps, soon to be. Age is irrelevant. Choose any number you wish, I will be so one day.'

'But you are Wilberforce, aren't you?'

The bird flew down and landed on Grandpa Jock's baldy head; its sharp claws digging into his skin.

'A journey of a thousand years begins with a single peck,' and the parrot snapped at the old man's ears and the ginger strands of hair wisping out at the sides. Grandpa Jock began running from side to side, trying to shoo the bird away but the parrot held on tightly. George could only follow, occasionally jumping up to swipe a hand at the bird but only succeeding in whacking his grandpa around the ear.

'Get off me, you flying butt-breath,' shouted Grandpa Jock, his eyes tight shut against the pecks and nibbles raining down on his head. Blinded, the old Scotsman ran hither and thither, staggering out of the throne room and onto the top of a temple terrace, where he bumped into a young woman kneeling on the ground.

Chapter 33 - Ancient Eejit

I'm just going to say Sunday 6th April, 51BC.
You don't need all that Egyptian calendar stuff again

'Death to Cleopatra!' shouted the ferocious man in the loin cloth and decorated headdress.

He was looking up to the sky, holding a vicious snake in one hand and a high priest's golden staff in the other. Perhaps he was looking for some divine wisdom or guidance from the skies but he had certainly not seen Grandpa Jock stumble into the young woman with a parrot attached to his head.

But George had. He could see the whole scene unfold from the doorway of the terrace. Grandpa Jock tumbling to the floor in front of the young woman, almost protecting her and the priest ready to thrust his snake downwards. Grandpa Jock was now in the firing line, or biting line.

George rushed towards the priest. The parrot flew up above their heads, and for a split second the priest was distracted, surprised by the bird. He stopped mid-thrust, the brown snake hissing madly in his hand, its head rearing backwards.

With a crash and a bash and a thump and whump, George threw himself headlong into the big man, who staggered back and fell to his knees, dropping both the snake and his staff. The blue Macaw swooped down, snatched the snake in its claws and flew off over the river. At the height of its arc, the parrot released the creature and it plummeted into the water.

'Thank you, young man,' whispered Cleopatra, and George blushed.

'I don't think we're out of this yet, lassie,' replied Grandpa Jock watching a squadron of Egyptian soldiers running towards them. They were carrying huge spears and each had a short-curved sword on their belts.

'Seize the princess! Kill the other two!' yelled the High Priest, fury spraying from his mouth.

'I am not a princess. I am the rightful Pharaoh and ruler of the Kingdom of Egypt. Stop where you are!' The young woman had now risen to her feet, and was holding her shoulders back, commanding respect. The soldiers stopped immediately.

'Kill them all, you fools,' demanded the priest. 'As High Priest of Osiris, I command you!' His eyes were flashing red and his fists were clenched tightly.

The soldiers were caught between the nobility and dignity of the young woman and the manic desperation of the man who controlled their fates in the afterlife. It was an impossible choice... if only they had a sign.

At that very moment, a large cow fell out of the sky and crushed the High Priest beneath the weight of 20,000 teabags. The soldiers dropped to their knees and began bowing and scraping on the dirt. The large crowd who had been watching this scene unfold also fell to their knees in prayer. The cow staggered to its feet, four legs going in different directions at the same time. George recognised the costume immediately.

'Get your face out of my butt,' shouted the front end of the cow.

'Get your butt out of my face,' yelled the back end of the cow.

George giggled, not quite sure if it was Kenny at the back and Allison at the front, or vice versa. Whoever was at the rear-end was probably hoping that there would be no more time-warp trouser trumpeting for a while.

'Behold, Hathor! The sacred goddess of the sky,' cried Cleopatra.

'They might've built the pyramids but these ancient Egyptians are not the brightest,' whispered George, nudging Grandpa Jock.

'I'm telling you, lad, it was the aliens that built the pyramids.' And Grandpa Jock winked back.

Cleopatra was striding around the temple platform, basking in the majesty of the mysterious sky-cow-god, and her people's belief that their Pharaoh was actually descended from the heavens too. She had picked up the High Priest's golden staff and was wielding it like a mighty wand. None of the soldiers, and certainly none of her subjects, would dare question her divine authority now.

After enough time had passed to allow her strength and majesty to seep into her audience, Cleopatra stepped back to the centre of the terrace, glanced at the 'sacred' cow just once and then whispered to George.

'Thank you again, young man, you have saved my life twice this day. How you were able to summon Hathor, Goddess of the Great Flood and Bringer of Life to the River Nile I will never know but I am in your debt.'

'It's blooming roasting in this suit,' squeaked the front end of the cow. Cleopatra pretended she heard nothing.

'The High Priest Ptolemy has been after my throne ever since my father died,' she went on.

'And your bottom stinks, being so close and all,' moaned the back end of the cow.

'And so, I will grant you any reward you wish,' Cleopatra continued, ignoring the cow noises, bowing her head slightly and tapping the golden staff on the marble floor.

'Begging your pardon.' Grandpa Jock had stepped forward, licking his hand and smoothing down his fluffy bits of hair with his own spit. 'You haven't seen any gold coins around here, have you? With his head on them?' Grandpa Jock put his hand on George's shoulder and pointed to his face.

'And Hathor, the Cow-God thing, over there, on the other side?'

'What a marvellous idea, old man!' announced the young Pharaoh. 'I shall create a fortune in gold coin, as a dedication to this day.' And at that moment, the blue and yellow macaw flew down and settled on top of her golden staff.

'Hey, look. It's Wilberforce!' shouted the front half of the cow, being the only part of the cow that could see.

'I can't look anywhere,' cried the back end. 'It's really dark in here and all I can see is your bottom.'

'Wilberforce, you say,' nodded the parrot. 'The old man mentioned that name before. And I rather like it.'

'So, you're not Wilberforce?' said George, puzzled.

'I am now,' replied the parrot.

But before George could figure out what the bird was talking about, there came a dreadful commotion from the river bank.

Beyond the terrace, down towards the Nile, they could see a small man in a green suit and hat, jumping in and out of the puddles yelping. He was clutching his bottom with both hands and looked to be in a great deal of pain. All the soldiers, the scribes, the craftspeople and all the other subjects had forgotten about their royal Pharaoh up on the terrace and had begun drifting down towards the water, keen to see the strange little man.

'Ow, ow, ow, ow, ow, ow, ow, OW, ow!' screeched the leprechaun. 'I beez bitten on the…'

'ASP!'

…laughed Grandpa Jock. 'That's what that type of snake is called. An asp.'

'Indeed, sir,' Cleopatra sighed. 'The Egyptian cobra is also known as an asp, and is one of the largest and most poisonous snakes in north Africa.'

'And remember, that Ptolemy guy was going to let it bite you,' smiled Grandpa Jock. 'You must repay him by becoming a wise and just ruler. When you wish good for others, good things come back to you. This is the law of nature.'

'You are indeed wise yourself, old man.' Cleopatra bowed towards the Scotsman. 'My people will be freed, to live together as a community, and they will judge me by my deeds and kindness. What man or woman will not follow when an Empress leads the way?'

'Thank you, your highness, but you really must excuse me, and perhaps stand clear...' bowed Grandpa Jock in return. 'I may be about to blow off a right royal rasper!'

Chapter 34 - Bubble, Bubble

Leprechaun time

'A right royal rasper?' giggled George 'You should be knighted for that one, Grandpa!'

'Did you see the look on that Pharaoh lassie's face?' laughed Grandpa Jock. 'She dropped her staff, and the feathers blew off the back of that bird.'

'I hope they're okay,' said George, looking around him. 'He looked a bit baldy.'

Grandpa Jock was standing in the darkness, holding his sides and chuckling uncontrollably. There was a little wisp of steam still floating out from underneath his kilt and tiny sparks danced across the floor. Beside a small pool and an even smaller puddle lay a mangled and smoking cow costume which was still kicking madly. Sitting quietly in the corner was a solid black cauldron, and perched on the top lip of the cauldron was a blue and yellow parrot.

'Well, I must say that you all took your time,' announced the parrot somewhat rudely. 'I've been waiting around here in this stupid cave for you lot for the last three days.'

Crayon Kenny had since lifted the back end of the cow suit from his head, and was standing by the pools with his cow trousers on. The cow's head and front legs were still staggering blindly around the cave.

'Hold on,' replied Kenny, having a think and scratching the inside of his nostril whilst he did it. 'We've only been gone twenty minutes.'

'Three days!' declared the parrot. Grandpa Jock was staring at the bird.

'Is your name Wilberforce?' he asked, raising a suspiciously bushy eyebrow.

'What? Seriously?' gasped Wilberforce. 'I only introduced myself to you on board that pirate ship a short while ago. Surely you haven't forgotten my name by now.'

To George, the pirate ship seemed like a lifetime ago, and Grandpa Jock nodded his own confusion. The front end of the cow bumped into the cauldron, whilst Kenny was ticking the events off on his fingers.

'We escaped the pirate ship,' he mumbled. 'We went back to Mr Jock's house with the treasure chest... and those blooming cats,' he went on. 'Then me and Allison put on that cow suit as a disguise, jumped into that pool of water over there... and... ' Kenny was growing in confidence the more he became certain of events.

'Hang on, you told us to jump into that pool of water over there, parrot!' he yelled. Wilberforce tucked his head under his wing. 'Then we landed on top of that priest geezer, Mr Jock dropped a whopper, and we jumped back here. We've only been gone twenty minutes!'

'A little help here please,' muffled the cow's head, bumping into the cauldron for a third time. George stepped over to the cow and began to pull its head off.

'That's it. He was right' gasped Grandpa Jock. 'Time is an illusion.'

'What are you on about, Grandpa,' shouted George over his shoulder, with the cow's head almost removed from Allison's shoulders.

'That Einstein scientist guy. The one with the fuzzy hair. Time moves at different speeds,' said Grandpa Jock. 'Like when time flies when you're having fun, or drags when you're bored.'

'Actually, Albert Einstein's theory of relativity does state that time is the fourth dimension,' nodded Wilberforce. 'And that the faster an object travels towards the speed of light, the slower time passes. So time travels at different speeds through different places, through different wormholes, you see?'

'No, not really,' groaned Kenny, sticking another reassuringly simple finger up his nose again. Life was always easier to understand with a finger up your nostril.

But life never wants to be understood for long; life loves complexity. And with a flash and a crash and a spiralling green vortex of noise and sound and a slight smell of sulphur, a leprechaun and a wooden chest came spinning out of the wormhole and landed with a thump against the far wall of the cave. The leprechaun sat up straight on top of the chest, shook his head, and as he did so, his lower jaw wobbled.

'You!' shouted the parrot, pointing a wing at the little green man.

'You!' shouted the leprechaun in return.

'You!' yelled George to Allison, as he pulled the cow's head off her shoulders, although he realised later that he knew Allison was in there and that he actually sounded pretty stupid.

'You!' shouted Wilberforce again.

'You? Who me?' asked Grandpa Jock, not really sure why everyone was shouting but just wanting to join in.

'No, him!' screeched the parrot.

'Me too,' shouted Kenny, not wanting to be left out. 'Hey, that's our treasure chest! From Grandpa Jock's house'.

'My treasure chest,' growled the leprechaun. 'And what are you all doing in my cave?'

'What are you doing with my treasure?' demanded George, pointing at the chest.

'This is my treasure,' snarled Tom. 'I beez collecting it for hundreds of years. You beez only helping me recently.'

'But each coin has the lad's face on it,' argued Grandpa Jock, taking a step towards the leprechaun.

'There is no point arguing with that littlo ruffian,' Wilberforce said. 'Greed is a fat demon with a small mouth and whatever you feed it is never enough.'

'And you beez the flea-bitten old bird that stole my golden treasure,' hissed the leprechaun.

Wilberforce replied, 'There are so many things wrong with that statement, please allow me to explain.' Kenny groaned and put his face in his hands.

'First of all, it was not your treasure to begin with, you've been stealing from other people for centuries. Secondly, I did not steal the gold from you, I merely distributed across time for anyone to find. And lastly, that gold was technically a dedication to George and erm... that cow thing, from Cleopatra for saving her life. The golden staff was forged and pressed into coins. I should know. I was there!'.

'Yes,' cried Grandpa Jock. 'You were there! Wilberforce, in Egypt, two thousand years ago. I knew it was you!' Grandpa Jock was delighted to know he was right at last.

'You are correct, Mr Jock. I am that parrot but not the same parrot as the one you see before you today. I didn't even know my name could be *Wilberforce* to begin with,' explained Wilberforce. 'You see, two beings, be they parrots or people or even leprechauns cannot be in the same place in the same time zone together... quantum physics would just not allow it.'

Kenny began to sob quietly. 'No, no, no, not that wibbly-wobbly stuff again.'

'But that was my beginning,' the bird continued. 'And your bottom blast gave me longevity. Once my feathers grew back, I journeyed through time for hundreds of years. Unfortunately I met this bog-trotting gobdaw, who tried to steal my yellow plumage, so I thought I would teach him a lesson.'

'You scattered the gold?' whispered George.

'Stole my gold,' hissed Tiny Tom.

'*Shared* that gold, and not yours,' nodded the parrot, smugly. 'Across history, I did spread that wealth, for nearly eighteen hundred years, until he banished me onto that pirate ship. It's no wonder I was hiding from that blasted leprechaun.'

'That means you're…' gulped George.

'Eighteen hundred years old,' gasped Kenny and Allison together. Allison was also relieved to be out of the cow costume. Kenny was just relieved to out of the bottom of the cow costume.

'So how old do yooz take me for?' growled the little man again, staring at everyone in the cave. 'Magic beez my curse, and magic will be your punishment. Start loading that gold into my crock.'

'And I should point out,' said the parrot, rather warily, 'that he does have a nasty curse in his magical little paws.'

'Nonsense,' cried Grandpa Jock. 'Irish people are always cursing, and usually in a nice way.' But as he stepped forward, Tiny Tom unleashed a furious volley of sparks and lasers and electrical volts from his fingers. Grandpa Jock was thrust backwards against the wall, where he slumped down unmoving in a heap.

'Grandpa!' cried George, running forward.

"Silence, foolish boy,' yelled the leprechaun. 'Stop there, turn around and start loading my gold into that there cauldron and I might let your ol' gran' pappy live!'

Chapter 35 - Toil and Trouble

George, Kenny and Allison continued to unload the coins from the different bags taken from around history, as well as from the treasure chest, and were throwing them casually into the cauldron. Occasionally, Tiny Tom would fire off a sparkle of leprechaun magic just to keep them on their toes, and the cauldron would frazzle too.

Wilberforce had flown over towards the pools where Grandpa Jock was lying motionless. The parrot would nudge the old Scotsman with his beak but there was no movement. All three children would glance across now and again but it seemed useless; Grandpa Jock was still.

The parrot was looking at Grandpa Jock but seemed to be talking to the children... at least one of them.

'Girl, girl,' whispered Wilberforce. 'Do you remember the quantum physics of gold? Do you remember about blue spectrum light?'

'This is no time for a chemistry lesson, bird-brain,' yelled the leprechaun. 'Keep filling that pot! And somebody needs to sook this snake poison out of my butt-cheek!'

'Think about blue spectrum life!' squawked the bird and flew up towards the roof of the cave, as the leprechaun fired another volley of electrons towards the parrot. Both George and Kenny noticed that after each bolt of electricity that left Tiny Tom's fingertips he began to breath heavily. He panted, he gasped and he took in lungfuls of air. Allison had stopped filling the chest and was turning a coin over in her fingers.

'Too much wealth is not good, child,' screeched Wilberforce from the top of the cave. 'Gold makes people even greedier. There is a reason why enough is enough.'

'Gold absorbs the soul,' whispered Allison. George and

Kenny turned to look at her, only Kenny now beginning realise. Allison turned one of the coins over in her fingers again. She flipped it towards the leprechaun and it struck him on the side of his face.

Tiny Tom screamed in pain, a beam of golden light shining out from the small cut on the side of his face.

'It burns,' he shrieked. 'It burns!'

Allison dipped her hands into the cauldron and pulled out a handful of coins. She threw them at the leprechaun and they jingled across the cave. Tiny Tom held up his hands against this golden onslaught and whimpered in distress as spikes of golden light flew from his body.

'Touching too much gold can burn out your soul, Tom,' squawked the parrot from above. 'I warned you about that… but you were too greedy.'

'You can't blame old Tom now, can you?' giggled the leprechaun, rubbing his hands against his face. 'I beez only having a bit of fun with you.' He was crawling backwards into the corner, as George and Kenny armed themselves with more coins.

'No, now, you can't be trapping a leprechaun, boys. We beez an endangered species, you know.' Tiny Tom was apologetic, truly afraid, and almost pitiful.

'Aye, endangered,' spat Grandpa Jock. 'I'm the one gonna endanger ye.'

Grandpa Jock was alive and well, and now standing by the pools, his hands clenched into large balls of muscle. The leprechaun might be using magic but Grandpa Jock knew he had grit and determination and belief on his side. He stepped towards the small green man.

'No, it's true,' yelped Tom, 'Leprechauns are an officially protected species under European Union law!'

'Technically, he is correct,' fluttered Wilberforce. 'The European Union does recognise leprechauns as an officially endangered species, and capture of such carries a £20,000 fine and six months in prison.'

The leprechaun stopped crawling and began to feel braver. George, Kenny, Allison and Grandpa Jock all stopped and Tiny Tom stood up.

'Now then, what to do, what to do?' growled the little man, drumming his fingers together mischievously. 'I'll be taking my gold, of course.'

But as he said this, more sparkles appeared in the corner behind the children. The legs on the cauldron began to stretch and little toes pushed their way out of the stumps. The cauldron sat upright and the gaping mouth of the pot seemed to yawn. The studs around its framework rattled and its legs began to dance widely on the spot.

'Is it coming to life?' gasped Allison.

'Gold affects more than just people,' squawked Wilberforce from the top of the cave. 'Perhaps best to stand back now, children.'

The cauldron was now spinning around on its toes, coins flying out in all directions and sparks flying. Tiny Tom was backing away in the corner of the cave again and coins flew out of the top of the pot, as if the cauldron was firing gold at the little man. He ducked furiously and backed further into the blackness.

Against the wall behind the leprechaun was a spiralling green vortex of energy and mass and velocity, spitting and spewing sparks and smells, until the very centre of the earth and the galaxy and the universe were fighting against each other. Gravity was an outside force and seemed to be winning when it pulled the little green man towards the black hole. Of course, the cauldron was a dark horse, with no previous experience, and nothing but raw power and might and rage on its side. And being a cauldron, it did not believe in abstract concepts such as gravity.

So, the cauldron lifted itself up onto its little steel toes and bombed after the leprechaun, hurtling its black iron body against the little man's heels, into the void of space and time and shiny, shiny lights.

Behind the cauldron, standing near the pool, away from the swirling vortex, someone farted. It might've been fear, it might've been beans but no one would admit to it afterwards.

It wasn't a big fart, it wasn't a greasy fart but it was a slippery little wisp of wind, just enough to blow open the fabric of space and time.

Chapter 36 - Greed

Present day

'Look at the state of my chair!'

The tired and tattered old armchair which had sat proudly in the corner of Grandpa Jock's living room, directly opposite the huge flat-screen TV, was now shredded and broken. Where once it was burst and battered, and held together with duct tape, the chair was now a pile of stuffing, fluff and worn material. Even the wooden structure beneath seemed to have been attacked by a herd of rhinos.

Two small, fluffy kittens were sleeping soundly on the sofa, curled up into little balls of innocence.

'What chair?' asked Kenny.

'There's not a lot of chair left, Grandpa,' added George.

Grandpa Jock knelt down beside the remains of his favourite piece of furniture and sniffed. A little bead of snot was dripping down to the tip of his nose but no amount of sniffing could bring it back up so he wiped it with the back of his hand.

'We had some great times together, didn't we?'

'Yeah, Grandpa. The pirates were cool, and Shakespeare, and all the other mad places. But those Aztec warriors were a bit scary,' said George, remembering his adventures.

'I'm not talking to you, lad. I'm talking to my chair,' sobbed Grandpa Jock, holding up bits of stuffing and rubbing them against his cheek. 'Who could've done this?'

Allison was now sitting on the sofa tickling the kittens behind their ears, and Mr Snuffles and Splat! purred softly in reply. God-like and serene, they were a picture of cuteness and calm.

'But what happened to that leprechaun?' asked Kenny, to no one in particular.

'I definitely saw the cauldron grow legs and come to life,' added George, and at that, a flurry of blue and yellow feathers fluttered into the living room. The kittens lifted their heads for a second but nodded back off to sleep again.

'Well, I hope you have all learned your lessons,' squawked Wilberforce bluntly. 'Don't talk to strangers. Don't take what doesn't belong to you and...'

'And don't let rancid parrots with sharp claws attach themselves to your shoulders,' interrupted Kenny, still rubbing the scratch marks around his neck.

'I was about to say that greed corrupts people. It makes men and women, and children for that matter, do bad things just because they want something, if they are desperate enough.' Wilberforce fluffed his feathers in a shiver of self-importance. 'Any material thing that you want is merely a symbol. You do not want it for itself, but because it will content your spirit for the moment... and only for a moment.'

'YA BEAUTY!'

Grandpa Jock was now dancing around the living room, kicking his legs and waving his arms about. His hand was humming with a golden glow.

'I've just found three of them golden coins under my chair!' he yelled. 'Finders keepers, losers weepers!'

He grasped the coins tightly in one hand as he tucked his thumb into his belt. He curled his right hand into an 'L' shape and placed it on his forehead, dancing back and forth, kicking his legs out to the side.

'LOSER!' he cried with delight.

'The finder's keeping, and the leprechaun's weeping!' laughed Grandpa Jock. 'I've been meaning to buy a new TV for a fortnight.'

'I thought you were needing a new chair,' asked George, puzzled.

'Yeah, and a new TV too. And it's gotta be one of those big gamer chairs,' blabbered Grandpa. 'With surround-sound speakers and a sub-woofer, and foot pedals and a harness, and a cup holder. It's gotta have a big cup holder.'

'Epic!' cooed Kenny.

'Awesome!' swooned George.

'Have you boys learned nothing?' asked Allison, putting her hands on her hips. 'Wilberforce has just been telling about the evils of greed, and you three start drooling over a new chair.'

'It is quite alright, young lady,' declared Wilberforce. 'I have been watching the human race for nearly two thousand years, and they have learned nothing from history. You will all continue to repeat your mistakes, just like the leprechaun.'

'What happened to him?' asked Allison. 'Where did he go?'

'Who knows?' shrugged the parrot. 'The cauldron's golden magic was very powerful, with all the coins absorbing so many people's hopes and dreams and desires. He could be anywhere throughout history.'

'Did you really scatter his gold across time?' asked Allison with a wry smile.

'Well, to be honest, it was the cauldron's idea,' smirked Wilberforce. 'And history always repeats itself.'

'History stinks!' said Kenny, butting in. Grandpa Jock had skipped off to the kitchen, leaving the boys in the living room.

'You weren't in London four hundred years ago, Kenny. With rivers of wee and poop and waste everywhere,' groaned George. 'Now that place really was absolutely honking.'

'See, so we have learned something, Wilberforce,' said Allison. 'We are better at looking after ourselves nowadays.

142

Better hygiene, better medicine…'

Wilberforce sighed. 'That's just painting over a poo. Human souls will still stink in the middle if kindness, respect and honesty are not at your core.'

Allison, Crayon Kenny and George stood in silence for a moment, allowing Wilberforce's words to sink in, before a wild yell from the kitchen interrupted their thoughts.

'Hey! There's still a little bit of curry left in this pot!' shouted the voice from the kitchen.

'As I said, they never learn,' sighed Wilberforce.

'Right, Grandpa,' called George. 'You behave yourself now.'

'Sure I will, lad,' giggled Grandpa Jock, walking through with a spoon held up to his mouth. 'I'll be as good as gold.'

The End

Epilogue

Well, little reader, I hope this story gave you all the adventure you were looking for. We had pirates, and parrots and plenty of parping. Aztecs, Egyptians and one or two cheeky moments of fun. Oh yeah, yeah, we had a few lessons from history too but we don't need to worry about that stuff. Who needs to learn about that?!

But here's the important stuff... no animals were hurt during the writing of this book. No kittens, no cows, no nothing!

And children - Do not load small kittens into catapults or any other firing devices. Or puppies! Or any other small animal, and that includes your little brothers and sisters.

So, in the end, the kittens were freed, the slaves were freed, Wilberforce was freed from the pirates, Mrs Mincewind was freed from something or other, hopefully her addiction to sugar.

And they all lived happily ever after...

(well, almost)

Translation: 'Those two are worth watching. They are close to discovering our secret.'
    'Don't worry. No one will believe them anyway.'

Quotes used to inspire this story

"We are too young to realise that certain things are impossible... So we will do them anyway."
– William Wilberforce

"The objects of the present life fill the human eye with a false magnification because of their immediacy."
– William Wilberforce

"A good head and a good heart are a formidable combination." Nelson Mandela

"Education is the most powerful weapon which you can use to change the world." Nelson Mandela

"There is no passion to be found playing small - in settling for a life that is less than the one you are capable of living"
- Nelson Mandela

"It always seems impossible until it's done."
– Nelson Mandela

"To believe a thing impossible is to make it so."
– French Proverb

"There is a sufficiency in the world for man's need but not for man's greed." – Mahatma Ghandi

"Whatever you love doing most, become really good at it and turn into your job. You'll get paid for having fun!"
– Stuart Reid

"Life throws challenges and every challenge comes with rainbows and lights to conquer it." Amit Ray

"So many of our dreams at first seem impossible, then they seem improbable, and then, when we summon the will, they soon become inevitable." – Christopher Reeve

"Sometimes I've believed as many as six impossible things before breakfast." – Lewis Carroll

"Any so-called material thing that you want is merely a symbol: you want it not for itself, but because it will content your spirit for the moment." – Mark Twain

Biography of William Wilberforce

William Wilberforce was a British politician known as the leader of the movement to stop the slave trade. Born in Kingston upon Hull, Yorkshire, in 1759, he began his political career at the age of just 21, eventually becoming a Member of Parliament for Yorkshire. In 1785, he became a Christian, which resulted in major changes to his lifestyle and a lifelong concern for social reform and progress.

In 1787, he joined a group of anti-slave-trade activists, who persuaded Wilberforce to take on the cause of abolition, and he soon became one of the leading English abolitionists. He headed the parliamentary campaign against the British slave trade for twenty years until the passage of the Slave Trade Act of 1807.

Wilberforce was convinced of the importance of morality and education. He championed causes and campaigns such as the British missionary work in India, the creation of a free colony in Sierra Leone, the foundation of the Church Mission Society, as well as the Society for the Prevention of Cruelty to Animals.

In later years, Wilberforce supported the campaign for the complete abolition of slavery, and continued his involvement after 1826, when he resigned from Parliament because of his failing health. That campaign led to the Slavery Abolition Act 1833, which abolished slavery in most of the British Empire.

Wilberforce died just three days after hearing that the passage of the Act through Parliament was assured. He was buried in Westminster Abbey.

About the author, Stuart Reid

Stuart Reid is 49 years old, going on 10.

Throughout his early life he was dedicated to being immature, having fun and getting into trouble. After scoring a goal in the playground Stuart was known to celebrate by kissing lollypop ladies.

He is allergic to ties; blaming them for stifling the blood flow to his imagination throughout his twenties and thirties. After turning up at the wrong college, Stuart was forced to spend the next 25 years being boring, professional and corporate. His fun-loving attitude was further suppressed by the weight of career responsibility, as a business manager in the retail and hospitality industries in the UK and Dubai.

Stuart is one of the busiest authors in Britain, performing daily at schools, libraries, book stores and festivals with his book event Reading Rocks! He has appeared at over 1,200 schools and has performed to over 250,000 children. In 2015 Stuart was invited to tour overseas, with visits to schools in Ireland, Dubai and Abu Dhabi, performing for 120 princes at the Royal Rashid School For Boys.

He has performed his energetic and exciting book readings at the Edinburgh Fringe Festival, has been featured on national television, radio and countless newspapers and magazines. He won the Forward National Literature Silver Seal in 2012 for his debut novel, Gorgeous George and the Giant Geriatric Generator and was recently presented with the Enterprise in Education Champion Award by Falkirk Council.

Stuart has been married for over twenty years. He has two children, a superman outfit and a spiky haircut.

About the illustrator, John Pender

John is 38 and currently lives in Grangemouth with his wife Angela and their young son, Lucas, aged 7.

Working from his offices in Glasgow, John has been a professional graphic designer and illustrator since he was 18 years old, contracted to create illustrations, artwork and digital logos for businesses around the world, along with a host of individual commissions of varying degrees.

Being a comic book lover since the age of 4, illustration is his true passion, doodling everything from the likes of Transformers, to Danger Mouse to Spider-man and Batman in pursuit of honing his skills over the years.

As well as cartoon and comic book art, John is also an accomplished digital artist, specialising in a more realistic form of art for this medium, and draws his inspiration from acclaimed names such as Charlie Adlard, famous for The Walking Dead graphic novels, Glenn Fabry from the Preacher series, as well as the renowned Dan Luvisi, Leinil Yu, Steve McNiven and Gary Frank.

John has been married to Angela for 7 years and he describes his wife as his 'source of inspiration, positivity and motivation for life.' John enjoys the relaxation and stress-relief that family life can bring.

Photography is another of John's pleasures, and has established a loyal and enthusiastic following on Instagram.

For Gorgeous George T-Shirts, Cups, Bags,
Notepads, Phone/iPad Cases and MANY other
products, please visit

http://www.redbubble.com/people/coldbludd/

collections/405936-gorgeous-george

THANK YOU!